Women of Passion

CLAUDETTE H. MCLENNON

EXPLORA BOOKS
700 – 838 West Hastings St. Vancouver, BC V6C 0A6
www.explorabooks.com
Phone: (604) 330 6795

ISBN: 978-1-997587-54-5 (*Paperback*)

978-1-997587-55-2 (*Hardback*)

978-1-997587-56-9 (*eBook*)

WOMEN

OF

PASSION

BOOK 1

Dedication

Dedicated to my siblings especially Janett, Alzie, my nieces and nephews, especially Jan, Yoki, Irvin and Shane. And to those like Evadney who have the audacity to boldly grasp their dreams and own their destiny.

Acknowledgement

Thank you, family and friends, for your belief, encouragement, well wishes as I press on to find a niche in the literary world. Your belief and confidence in my ability is a boost to navigate the competitive world of writing and to boldly explore avenues of possibility while believing in Matthew's 19:26 "With God all things are possible."

Contents

Preface

Martha "Marte" Renee Chimes was given 30 years for the murder of Judge Carle Banning Frondes. She was twenty-five when she was convicted and given thirty-years to life with the option of parole in twenty years. She was innocent but, a prominent and eligible Judge was murdered and someone needed to pay. The Governor and Mayor wanted a conviction, and she was it. Formerly a teen model and social worker she was confident she would be acquitted so they (she and friends) could continue working to rid New York of pedophiles. What of her children; the one adopted(girl) and the other (boy) stolen and what of the organization she founded WASP (Women Against Sexual Predators). Can she survive; or does she have the strength to continue the fight for her freedom?

Chapter 1

This is her first trip to the parole board. Would it be favorable? She was serving time for murder. It never failed to grip her in the stomach. She never believed she'd be convicted. They never found the murder weapon that caused Judge Banning to bleed out due to extensive internal bleeding. She saw the murderer- a teenager girl but was unwilling to give a full description as she was confident, she would not be convicted. Her empathy was with the child forced into sex and other atrocities and she suffered. If the good you do live after you then she is preserving her children that someday someone may rescue her too, if necessary.

Unconsciously Martha suddenly lapsed into reflection of her life. She hoped to be a model one day like Naomi Campbell or Shari Belafonte and Heidi. She is not exceptionally tall, but she had hopes. She had done head shots by age fourteen. Her parents were not thrilled but Grandpa Wesley gave her the money. She dared not try for Wilhemina. It was a tough agency for the very young to get in, she heard. Her parents insisted she get her education first without realizing many fashion models start as teenagers. Still, she had her dreams but to placate her parents told them she wanted to be a dietician. Well, if she is going to be a model, food and nutrition are very important part of everyone's life. Everyday there was a new weight loss gimmick. She had a choice of Lehman College in Bronx or Queens College, none of which held any thrill for her. She did not like

Brooklyn but that was a different story. She had heard too many tales of the professors there. But getting a catalog from Brooklyn College appeased her parents. By the age of fifteen she got many modelling calls, but some of them were too seedy and her mother objected. Well, her mother objected to just about everything, the makeup she had to wear, the styles.

She remembered getting an agency Trevor Rasi so he could sift through so she could sift through the undesirable offers. She remembered when she did her first shoot for Macy's Summer catalog. That was in December. Her teeth chattered the whole time. Why couldn't they have done it in Summer? But a winter photo shoot in New York is still winter. They plied her with hot tea and cocoa to stop her chattering teeth and to prevent her from turning blue. Well Macy was the first step. She had hopes and exceptions. After that first shoot, she and friends went to celebrate. They were all under age so they took the bus to Kings Plaza, disappointed that neither of them owned a car. But they would have dinner and a movie. It was a wonderful evening. They saw James Bond movie Golden Eye. They were on such a high that night! She could see her big break. At the shoot she met Ogwin Jackall. If she had been older and wiser she would've known to steer clear of him. His name said it, Jackall.

She was flattered by his interest as his eyes roved over body, every delicate curve and promising pulsating morsel of deliciousness. He openly appraised her body and when she blushed and pulled on a robe. He said how blessed she was to have such a magnificent curvaceous body. After that she met him again at the party of Mike Palance Director of photo shoot. They exchanged phone numbers then and afterwards dated. No matter, he was older than Max and Jason paled in comparison. Not that there was anything other than friendship between them but suddenly she felt all grown up compared to her friends. She started drifting away and lost the closeness they once shared. They hung out at school but at home, Ogwin took her to sophisticated clubs. Of course, her mother never knew, and she used the girls as alibis. Barbara objected to being used and she felt they were jealous of her because she was dating a real man not a schoolboy with their clumsy sweaty palms.

She was at a different party every week and she managed to put off going all the way with Ogwin stating many times the female issue. Sometimes when he caught on, she'd say it was the last day or it was too close and feared getting pregnant. Ogwin took her places, and they ended up on another photo shoot together. She was in silhouette but what did it matter? She loved what she was doing and most of all was with Ogwin. Her grades began to slip, and her parents grounded her. So that weekend she had to stay home she told Ogwin her grandmother was visiting from Westchester and the whole family would be there. She said she had a special bond with her grandmother Ethlyn. Well, her grandmother did come, and she was glad of the excuse. She is dating a man for heaven's sakes! How could she let on she was grounded? She wanted Ogwin to think of her as mature. He assumed she was 18 years old and did not correct him. The first time she went to club SOB she was frightened. He had to tell her to relax. The place was dark and smoky from all the cigarettes. They found a table a little way from the thick smog. When someone who had too much to drink started to make a ruckus, they left before the police got there.

She was glad to get out of the cloying hot space. The air outside felt heavenly. Besides she likes the village you never know which celebrity maybe strolling down 14th St. or the avenues. They strolled in the village passing a few homeless people. Ogwin was parked some four blocks away and she was happy she had walked with a pair sandal and traded her white Sam Libby pumps. That night she came close to losing her chastity. But by some miracle they were interrupted by sirens. She was glad for the interruption. Ogwin was getting more persistent. They quickly made their way to the car after that. The siren, although a part of city life, always signaled doom for her. Someone almost always gets hurt.

As they drove away from West Houston St., she silently thanked the siren. Furthermore, she was not the kind of girl to be groped or have her first intimate experience in a car luxurious or not. Yes, the Lexus is a prestigious car but still a car. Plus, her parents would have a fit if they knew Ogwin was 22 years to her mere 15 years. Being academically gifted had its perks. She was ahead of her grade and so many assumed she was older than she was. She never dissuaded them and found it rather advantageous. Her air of self of confidence worked well. She was told a long time ago about the birds and bees, at age 10 or so. She remembered how embarrassed her mother was and especially for an RN. She was sure she did that at Brownsville clinic where she worked at Saratoga Ave. But I guess with your own child it's awkward. She digested the information and remembered the emphasis her mother put on the marital bed.

Again, regret and pain stabbed her heart when she remembered the grief her mother felt. Poor mom! RN Dorette Marie Drayton Chimes and Clifton Barry Chimes, her parents. Her mother never really changed my name and went by both. It was hard on her parents, her sentencing. Her mother wailed how she would miss her, not see her married or have children. That was a whole other matter. She had a child, or rather children her mother didn't know about and, for the first time, admitted what a mess she had made of her life, all the secrets! This subterfuge, the dishonesty! and worst of all the betrayal. How did life go so wrong? Salem Baptist Church was right there at the corner of E 21st and Albemarle Rd. She was right there on a 18th St. Saint Paul's just on the other side. As she grew into a teenager, she became cynical of the church. There were too many gossipers, it would have been easy to go to the Adventist church, but she rejected that as hypocritical. It would just be a convenience nothing spiritual or biblical drove that thought. No, she didn't want to mingle with people who only became righteous and pious Friday evening and devil the rest of the week. Mr. Dellquest was the perfect example with his food caked false teeth. How does one forget to brush one's teeth. And all this time she was righteous, dishing out judgement. She was exactly like those she disdained.

All this is irrelevant. Why did this pop in her head? Over the years she had gained favor with the guards and office personnel. Once she made it plain to the other inmates, she was serving life for murder she had nothing to lose they backed away. They could not know how desolate she felt. She had lost everything; mother, father, sisters Yvonne, Gabrielle and brother Jonathan Calvin. She had stopped them making the quarterly trips after five years because she knew what a strain it was. What can you possibly say to someone serving life. How do you encourage him especially if that person doesn't want to fight; that there are psychological reasons but, she has a secret to hide. She wanted to protect that little girl. She snorted in disgust and her mind went back to all those years.

She'd dodged Ogwin advances for months. When he professed dying love for her and said it was his birthday she agreed reluctantly. The wine gave her the courage she lacked. What the fool! What a fool she was. How did she fall for such a wimpy ploy. He had his needs and the way he felt tense and uptight was a direct result of the lack of sexual release. He was going crazy. He loved her passionately. Wow! Soon she began to think he really loved her when he told her he knew she was a virgin and that she didn't want to pressure her. He understood he said of course he didn't. The change in him, the tactics worked. He was so solicitous. He was attentive always telling her how much he loved her- wined and dined her; dinner and the movie or he just took her dancing. He began taking her among his friends. And life was good. She had a great time really and that's when it happened.

She aired her fears about virgins getting pregnant at first encounter and he blew this aside. She begged him to use a condom, and he said he would after their first time. That was when she should have walked away but she believed he really loved her. She met his mother and siblings. That she convinced herself must mean something. She built a rapport with his sister Jill. They genuinely liked each other, and they hung out together, she even introduced her to the other partners of the Dynamos. Lull in a sense of false security she overlooked that he had an excuse for not having condoms on hand. She begged him and he agreed he would. It took a while for her to realize he had no intention of using condoms and she stopped him one night. No, she was adamant, no glove, no love. She told him she was waiting for a big shoot in two months, and she didn't want anything to mess it up. That was the first big quarrel they had. She reminded him he cannot get pregnant, so she had to protect herself.

At that point she went to a GYN to get fitted with an IUD and discuss the pros and cons. It was then she learned it was too late. She was pregnant. She challenged the doctor, so she did a blood sample. She had an appointment for the following week. She hoped and prayed that the urine test was a mistake. She prayed to the God she was too busy for but, no luck. She was pregnant. She cried in that lady's office she had to cancel her last two appointments. She was inconsolable. She couldn't tell her parents and worst that swimsuit shoot was coming up in the Bahamas. She would get to stay at the Atlantis. And they said possibly go on to Jamaica in Negril where the sand was white. She needed that photo shoot to enter the big leagues. This was her opportunity; she just couldn't give it up.

Chapter 2

Doctor James assured her she would be fine that nothing would be showing in six weeks that she can have the shoot and then decide what she wanted to do. After what seemed like an eternity, she left Doctor James' office and walked about downtown Brooklyn. She did not want to go home. She was angry, lonely, frustrated and mad as hell! What she feared the most happened. She decided to explore Metro Tech. What was FDNY doing there? She saw the park where the summer concerts were held and little cafes. There was a big Chase Bank and numerous places she didn't know exist; There telephone company was no more! Flatbush extension was crazy- had four lanes of traffic. For the first time Macy held no appeal. She loved Jamaican patties but not today. She smelled the Curry chicken; she longed for a roti and Curry chicken. She walked around, circled the court buildings, the Borough President's office and sat in the park. She ignored the whistles and made her way to the Marriott to freshen up, you just had to look as if you belonged. She rode the escalator veered from the conference rooms head toward the restaurant then veered to the bathroom. She took out her compact and dabbed at her face. Her eyes were red and puffy. She wet paper towels and rest on the lids. It was too dark to wear dark glasses so she gave herself smoky eyes and if anyone asked about her eyes she'll just lie about her contacts. Well, they wouldn't know she didn't wear glasses.

Hunger gnawed at her and finally she bought beef patties. She was very hungry. She went home and headed for her room. She declined dinner and took a shower. She struggled to forget what the doctor said. Well, she has to tell Ogwin but how? She is going to plead a headache when he calls to pick her up. Resentment rose in her. She is mad at him and more so herself. She should have sought an IUD before. Men never get pregnant! How often did she lament the fate of girls leaving school prematurely to have babies and curtail their high school goals. Now here she is in a similar situation. Martha, Martha she chided. That was a silly move; you have plans, aspirations, you have goals. You cannot be a Top Model like Naomi C, Tyra B or Heidi K. There are shoots to exotic places Hawaii, Aruba, Paris and Bonn. How did she lose focus to such an extent that she is in this predicament? If there's an upside, she should graduate in three months. Thankfully she did Regent's exam and was already enrolled in Brooklyn College and was doing two electives towards her Dietician degree. Truth be known, it was only two liberal arts studies (LAS) she was doing; Intro to Psychology and In Search of Wellness.

The call came after she fell asleep. The fact that she slept was a surprise to her. Voice sleepy and raspy she didn't have to plead headache to Ogwin. It was accepted and he even sounded genuinely concerned. What would he be like when she told him of her pregnancy? Will he be as understanding; will he shoulder his responsibility or be just another good time Charlie. Time will tell she reasoned. She refused to anticipate trouble and tried to push her dilemma from her. She spoke with Barbara who said she was staying home tonight preferring to go partying Saturday night. With forced enthusiasm she told Barbara she would be there. Martha looked at herself in the mirror with a critical eye, there was no bulge. She is flat as sheet cake. She made-up her mind she would be on that shoot to the Bahamas. Nothing would stop her not even wild horses. She needs to be careful of everything.

Two weeks later. When Bahamas looked like this Statue of Liberty, she chickened out of telling Ogwin. She told him she had Regents to study for. And math was kicking her in the derriere and needed to do the extra work. He gave in. She appeased him later that week. She quizzed him about growing up, of his dreams. Did he dream of being a model? When will he marry. And if he wanted children? He said he sees himself as a model, although he fell into it. He was at the right place at the right time. He was by South St. Seaport and some guys were shooting a video for a GAP commercial and he ended up as an extra. Later he used the video. To get him an interview with Liam's modeling agency, he started working out and working on his image. At 5 feet 10 inches, he worked especially hard. He was told that he has the IT factor. He looks great in water pictures, although he coveted the Armani and Versace suits and hopes one day he will get to model the top designers like Ford, et al. He does a lot of catalog shoots but hopes going to Willamina will put him on the top for all to see. He has no plan to marry anytime soon. He is too young to marry. He wants to focus on his modeling. He wants to make the cover of GQ. "Kids! he said. Eventually I want a son to carry on my name, but marriage and children are complications, I don't need now." Nothing should derail him or his plans if he wants to be regarded as a Top Model. Very few persons recognize him except in Bedford Stuyvesant where he grew up.

Martha digested the Information because suddenly she realized she didn't know much about him. She smiled grimly. What would he say when he finds out he's already a Papa? That growing inside her is a child they both conceived with effort she forced, a gaiety she did not feel. She wished fervently that the Bahamas shoot was over. She was tired of hiding her unhappiness and the only bright spot she would graduate with a Regency diploma. So, the few months before the end of school could not come fast enough, she looked forward to. It now as a Lord.

Something else to frustrate her. She is going crazy as her mother insists on going with her to the Bahamas. It's either she goes as a chaperone, or she didn't go. She promised she would not interfere or intrude. She pleaded, pouted and cried. She was not a baby. Her mother agreed but said she is 16 and therefore a child. In the end, she reluctantly agreed, but she really had no choice. She could sense doom, looming ahead. She had a fore sense her modeling career was dead. She needed this outing and the photo shoot for posterity. She always liked children and wanted children, but not now. She did not want to raise a child by herself. She felt her bubble boil inside her, almost suffocating her. She does not like abortion, and it seems that it would be her only unpleasant recourse. No one should have an abortion for abortion's sake.

She cried often. She does not know how she will live with the guilt of abortion, when her life is not in jeopardy. She did not see a way out. She hated the idea of being a single parent, yet she cannot tell her parents. Maybe she could tell grandmother, but then what? Even now there is nothing to see. Maybe three months before there'd be any indication of pregnancy. Now she knows lying and cheating are not for her. Guilt is a horrible accuser. She couldn't make up her mind when to tell Ogwin. He is a father. If she could guess his reaction, maybe she would know which course to take. In the end, she decided not to do prom, but go on the photo shoot and have a wonderful time because after that, her life is over. She would tell him after this shoot. However, she would feel less guilty if she miscarried or suffered a spontaneous abortion. Could she successfully contrive the situation? She will explore the possibility of how best to bring about a plan. She liked the possibility and decided to spend the next days with her friends.

She accepts she has a crush on Aquin. An infatuation. She regrets sleeping with him. Damn him, the way he was casual about marriage and children. She knew she was doomed and above all, only has herself to blame. Dumb! Dumb! she chided herself. When that young Adonis refused to use condom the first time, she should have run a mile. She should have run like Flo Joe. Now it's too late and bombarding her brain with guilt and recrimination is counterproductive. It is no use praying either. Her parents' words came back to haunt her; disobedient children always pay because the Bible say children, obey your parents, for this is right.

Martha shook her head. Reflecting on past sins had become a favorite pastime since the upcoming parole hearing. She could not deal with the recrimination. It seemed everyone knew what she did, although she knew no one knew anything about her private life. The only one who knew of the botched abortion was Ogwin and the quack that did it. She often wondered if it was because Ogwin was cheap and trying to save money, why she ended up with Boris Votyen? His nationality was the only thing she believed was genuine. Being a doctor? No- he said because of limited English worked as a nurse but is a doctor in his native Bosnia. Of course you are, she thought sarcastically. And I will marry royalty one day.

What he gave her did not exactly work. She went in and out of consciousness. At one point she heard voices but could not distinguish the words. At times she felt as if she was floating. During the ordeal, it seemed she was watching herself on the narrow Gurney. She noticed the place didn't look that sanitary from her view above. Actually, it looked dingy. Doctor Boris, his face red and sweating profusely, didn't inspire confidence as well as his hands were shaking. As he inserted the plastic (speculum she learnt later) and forced her open. She screamed. Then he removed that and inserted another plastic cylinder, and she lost consciousness at that point. When she came to, she was bleeding and in pain. There was a nurse maybe with red hair bending over her, telling her to wake up. She was hoarse and crying. What had she done? Even if the child was the size of a prawn, what had she done? How could she? No amount of confession could ease conscience and her shame. What would her mother and father say? She would not be able to look anyone in the eye. She was a first-class hypocrite. Didn't she profess to love babies? Didn't she babysit for the tenants in 1900, what if everyone aborted babies? Then there would be no world.

Why didn't she satisfy with her Bahamian trip? It was successful even with her mother there. True to her word, she did not intrude, although she was present a couple of times on the set. Neither her mother nor anyone noticed any change in her form. Why didn't she just hope and pray that evidence of her misdeed would stay hidden until after graduation? Then she should have gone somewhere quietly and have the baby. What if she was carrying twins? She hoped fervently that it was only one baby. She would go crazy. She could not carry that guilt. She didn't ascribe to abortion for abortion's sake, but genuine reasons, her own subjective reason. She would not sacrifice the life of the mother for the child or force a woman to birth a child of incest or rape. What if she never conceived again?

It was bad enough having sexual relations with a 22-year-old man, but abort a baby because it is inconvenient when there is a viable alternative? She did not even tell her mother. How low could she go? Ogwin would have to satisfy his needs elsewhere. He wanted no responsibility for their unborn child, and she did not relish the role of a single mother or parent. But the next man that ever get close has to have a ring, a fat wallet and a love that draped her like halo. She marveled how quickly she learned to despise Ogwin. She flatly refused to sleep with him. She learned the hard way; what they did was have sex. They did not have intimacy, or they'd be caring and affection.

She was oblivious to the rounding of her stomach because she was so angry and bitter. Then one day she asked Ogwin to take her to see Dr. Boris. His office turned out not to be his office but had used a rented space. Now she knew for sure he was doing illegal abortions. Now she was in a pickle. She was embarrassed to go back to Dr. James. She had to find a clinic and go incognito. She became afraid. Was the abortion not completed? Her breasts certainly looked fuller. She went to Kings County Satellite Clinic on Bristol Street. She wore contact lens, covered her head and wore dark glasses. She told the reception she was a student at Jefferson High and wanted to know if she was pregnant. All the time she talked, she kept her lids lowered, only lifting her head occasionally. She wanted to convey timidity, bashfulness, and innocence all rolled in one. Would the nurse buy it? For what seemed like an eternity she waited. And then she saw the Nurse Practitioner. The tears she shed that day were genuine tears for stupidity, regret and remorse. She was hysterical. The NP was gentle and understanding. She figured it was a secret she shared with no one, least of all her parents. The NP spoke softly, and her eyes were filled with compassion as she confirmed she was pregnant. She fainted. When she came to NP Patrick asked her if she had attempted an abortion as she noticed scarring which looked like tears and not fully healed. Her lie and life were about to unravel. She cunningly gave Precinct 71 phone number and address. They could contact the precinct, but she would not find her as Facie Santana did not exist. She thanked the NDP and ran despite the attempts to keep her.

She took the number three train and decided to take a ride in Manhattan. What a mess. First, she was pregnant, then she wasn't. Then she had an abortion, and it didn't happen. Now her reproductive organs were messed up and she's still pregnant. She laughed and cried. What a hot pile of- she halted her thoughts. Her mother hated vulgarity. Well, she was in a mess. Now did Ogwin know that the butcher didn't do the job right? She would not put herself through that again. She remembered the bleeding. They did not want to go to Planned Parenthood because there was always a group protesting there, shaming abortion seekers and it is too loud. Moreso, they did not want to be recognized or be associated with anyone. None of that mattered now she had to make a decision. Should she tell the sperm donor? She still could not see herself as a mother. A mother is a caring and nurturing. She was a kid, longing to confess to her mother to let her mother put her arms around her and tell her everything is going to be alright. Here she is, a child grappling with an adult situation. What must she do? She could tell her grandmother, Ethlyn, but she didn't want to compromise her in keeping her secret. Neither did she want to cause a rift in the family, because it certainly would. She was forced to admit that being so desperate to become a model had her mind twisted. She had become a me, myself and I person. Seeking and expecting adulation and special favor, she forgot what basic love and kindness was, thinking of others. She was growing up very fast.

She decided to get off the train at Times Square. She'd go walking-Maybe she'd end up at Madame Toussant or would go see a movie at the IMAX theater. She needed distraction. Her thoughts were chaotic, not friendly or comforting. Well, maybe she'll see a street performance. Many times, these impromptu, informal performances were entertaining and most showed the talent. Sometimes they'd be the exception where someone was making a fool of himself. She smiled as she remembered this man singing on the #4 train. Singing was not his friend, and he was horrible. Most everyone cringed in that car. The combined expressions said give it up. After one very long, torturous song, he held out his hat. Naturally he was ignored. He then said if he got nothing he would sing again and the whole car dived into their pockets to pay him. With those generous tips, he moved to the next car to torture the unsuspecting commuters. She remembered how she laughed that evening. She really loved public transportation. You were treated to a free pantomime. There were some earthy things that were said, revealed and seen. She endeavored to lose herself in 42nd St. Maybe she'd go to a theater and take in a show.

That revelation earlier was too hot to handle. Much too hot to handle. Her mind was in a vortex. Where can she go or what can she do? How is she going to get out of that predicament? She was angry that after the pain, bleeding and out of body experience, she was still pregnant. How can she possibly care for a baby? She didn't know what to do. Babysitting is so different. You are not in charge 24 hours a day. You do not have to find answers. What would her mother do? The shock would kill her. Her dad would be devastated. Why did she have to remember her parents now? Guilt was a heavy master she could not shake. She felt like such a hypocrite. Oh, can't she face her aunties and uncles and worst her cousin Charlotte. There was little love lost between them. Her aunt Ella had married a cardiologist. So financially they were comfortable. So, she was the Prima Donna. Her father, Doctor Sean Tudore doted on her. Martha was not envious of her, but there was an unspeakable rivalry. Academically, they were. peers, although she went to Catholic school, while she went to Midwood High, a top school in Brooklyn. Boy, was she in trouble big time. Goodness, she was almost dizzy with all the thoughts swirling in her mind. Now Charlotte would one up her.

Oh, Lord Jesus. I know I've not been what you require us to be, but please get me out of this mess. Please help me. I have no one to turn to. Help me. She cried in silent tears. Help me. She switched to the number one train and went to Columbus Circle and Central Park and walked around. Maybe she can find answers. Maybe God hears her prayer. Maybe He doesn't care, she had grumbled against going to Flatbush Tompkins Congregational Church. She likes the building and the surrounding area, especially in spring and summer. She wished she had paid more attention to Reverend Dean Fisher. She pushed her aside, her thoughts with effort, and strolled into the grounds of Central Park South. She became aware of someone watching her. She saw an older man openly watching her. She rolled her eyes, instantly angry. Other times, she would be amused, but not today. The way he is looking at her as if she is a takeout meal. What is she, a Mickey D's Happy meal? She prays no one says anything to her. She is more than willing to heap all of her stress and strain on anyone, male or female, young or old. She inhaled deeply; she walked leisurely and then sat pensively away from a family. There was a pretty baby girl, about 18 months. It was obvious she had just discovered running. Her parents took turns chasing her, much to her delight. As soon as she was brought back to the blanket, she took off again. She was laughing and very happy as shrieks of delight caught Martha's ears. She watched as the father tossed her in the air and caught her. It was such a beautiful setting- Ideal. She felt something crawling on her cheeks, and as she brushed it away impatiently, she saw her hand was wet. Up to that point, she didn't realize she was crying. Watching that family brought home what the baby she was carrying would never have; never know.

She pulled a paper napkin from her bag and she dabbed her cheeks Next; the little girl was inches away from her. She held out her hand with a veggie stick. Her parents' mouth slightly agape, looked on. Martha graciously accepted the gift, thanking her. The mother came over and said Jordan (the baby's name) has never done that, not with strangers. Jordan proceeded to sit beside Martha. She smiled at Jordan. She was chunky, with pink cheeks and laughing gray eyes. With little encouragement, Jordan sat in Martha's lap. The mother's eyes bulged, and she apologized. Martha assured her it was no trouble. She babysits when not in school and Jordan must know that.

"I am Marty," she said.

I'm a Rebecca and my husband Stan."

"I'm so pleased to meet you. You have a beautiful daughter. She is adorable and delightful."

"Yes, she is. You forget energetic though. They all laughed.

"We had given up trying when we found out we were pregnant. Five years! You see, she's, our miracle. I heard the whisper of that baby for so long. Our next step was to a fertility clinic, but thank heavens we didn't have to," said Rebecca.

"Oh, my goodness. This is so wonderful. I am so happy for you," said Martha enthusiastically.

"Okay, Jordan. Time to go. You should sleep well tonight."

As they took their leave, Jordan started to fuss to be put down. Once down, she turned towards Martha and ran to her and kissed her cheek. The only one not surprised was Jordan.

"I think you bewitched my daughter. She is a happy child, but cautious around strangers except you."

"Well, she stole my heart. Never met anyone like her," Martha said softly.

As they said goodbye, she felt a tug in her heart. And before her flashed a vision of a child running with ponytails and shrieking, much like Jordan was. She wept. After that she knew what she would do. She would give the baby up for adoption. Hearing how long Rebecca and husband tried for a child; here she is pregnant without trying and undecided what to do. What an irony. She is 16 and knows right from wrong well, her mother always said. No matter what you do in darkness, it will come to light. That is true. Nobody knows. Or at least she doesn't believe anyone knows she is sexually active. Maybe she is delusional and the whole world knows. Maybe her baggy clothes are fooling no one. She sighed. She went to sleep that night with a picture of Jordan with her parents. How beautiful. She also saw the vision of brown baby running with ponytail.

Chapter 3

Her sleep was troubled. She dreamed she was fighting with Ogwin. She also dreamed that she told her parents and were promptly disowned. She cried, asking them to forgive her. She repeated. I am sorry. I'm sorry until she felt arms shaking her.

"You are talking in your sleep" her mother said.

Oh. What was I saying? Martha asked warily.

"Well, you were saying I am sorry, I am sorry, pleading, her mother said. You have been looking peaky. Are you feeling alright? Think maybe you should see the doctor?"

"I'm fine, mom. You are seeing things, but thank you, she added softly to take the sting out of her response to see the doctor. No, Doctor Freda Cummings will not be seeing her anytime too soon, if ever, she thought vehemently. She would do the next best thing. She'll go visit Grandma Ethlyn and stay for two weeks, leave for home but would go to Mount Vernon. She would let her parents know she is okay, but she'd have the baby and give him or her up for adoption. She had made some bad choices in her 16 years. Now, she is not only a teen mother but a runaway as well. She would emerge the following year. She would transfer credits to Lehman College in the Bronx. The number four and D trains would take her there.

When she got home. He showered and hit her room. She told her mother she was sleepy and not hungry as she ate outside. Mentally exhausted, she climbs into the bed and pulls the sheet over her head.

She is not in the mood to talk in person or on the phone. She turned off her phone. Surprisingly, she slept. Today is when she must make concrete plans. She will search the New York Times and Daily News for adoption agencies and to see what apartments are available and where she needs to put distance between herself and Brooklyn. But one thing was unchanged. She will continue her college education, she is adamant. Nothing will stop her. She must defy the odds. Her earnings from modeling will carry her through college. With kindness of faith, she will encounter no one she knows or vice versa. She is grateful for meeting Rebecca and Stan and Jordan. What a delightful baby. But what did it take to get Jordan to that point. She babysits, but that is because it is temporary. She copes but, with full time she balks at the idea. Me a mother? She is terrified. She knows what biology says, but that is all abstract. She knows labor and delivery is no joke. Just thinking about it, her knees feel weak and her stomach hurts. Beads of perspiration cover her brow and top lip. Why Lord? Can't you fix this? I love babies when they belong to someone else. I do not want to be a teenage mother. She wished she could turn the clock back. And resentment rolls so high it almost blocked her breathing. She resented Ogwin. He got a butcher to abort the baby who is still here. And now she may never conceive again yet she cannot have a baby now.

Is she being selfish? All the bad chat and sass flowed back to her loud and shouting. Why is her conscience so active? She is tired of quietening her inner voice. She is tired of fretting when the baby gets older then everyone will know. She is embarrassed and ashamed. She is guilty as she betrayed everything her parents taught her and her three siblings. Jonathan Calvin. Yvonne Angella, and Denise Gabriella Chime. They are younger than she is and therefore cannot confide in them. For the first time she realized that being the first born is not an advantage. She wished she had an older sister. She has so many questions. She's reading as much as she can about pregnancy but undercover to avoid anyone knowing. She feels like a hypocrite. She has not confided in Sophia,

Barbara or Stephanie. She's afraid of what they may think of her. She lost the closeness she once enjoyed with the guys. She ditched them when she started seeing Aquin. Now she's alone. Can't her mother of her dilemma. Doesn't want to jeopardize Grandma Ethylene's relationship with her parents. She thought of taking Auntie Norma or maybe Auntie Jean in her confidence. She could see the fight with her parents and separations. She couldn't do that. She wished she had shared. Their phone number with Rebecca and Stan. I cannot get my two aunts in the middle of this mess. She has to handle it herself. She has to make this right. Maybe she can contact the Catholic Charities. Would they help her without contacting her parents? Or would they insist on it? She can pretend to be a runaway or tell she is contemplating an abortion. They wouldn't know she attempted to and failed. And has no plans to try again.

This is a heavy price for deception. She hopes she has an accident where she miscarries. So, it's not a nudge to her conscience. She is contemplating a crime, she tells herself. She isn't doing anything to precipitate any accident. Isn't that why it's an accident? She will not help it, but it would solve all her problems. She remembered her mother chiding her friend that what you think about, you bring about. It is like Job. She did not see the connection, but the thoughts are powerful. The battle raged inside her as she vacillated between fatalism and hope. This is a lesson she will not soon forget.

As the days turn to weeks and weeks to months. She ditched Brooklyn and headed for Mount Vernon. She left her mother a note with a promise to keep in touch. She could not believe her fortune that even at six months pregnant, there was barely a bulge. And that's when she left, not wanting to tempt fate. Plus, she was unhappy and lived on her nerves waiting for her parents to find out. She wished they had. The first thing she will tell a teenager do not get pregnant if you have strict parents, grow up in the church, and have a delicate conscience. Guilt will eat you alive. You undergo a tsunami of guilt. It was almost physical. So as not to feel a total heel and jerk, she called her girlfriends Barbara, Sophia and Stephanie and told them she's leaving but cannot tell them why; but maybe someday in the future. She gave each of them a Pandora bracelet. For a time when they were Brooklyn Divas AKA BD. She swore them to secrecy about her leaving but didn't want to drag them into her world of deceit. She really loved them. She called Jason and Max and said goodbye and she left.

She worked through the local diocese to have the baby adopted. She appeased her conscience and did not wish harm to the baby. In the midst of her upheaval, she heard her Pastor clearly in her mind, Jesus said, Suffer the little children to come unto me. Outrageous, she thought. Well, whether by abortion or otherwise, wouldn't they still go to him? She shook her head. She was getting violent. Then she realized she was bitter. But as she acknowledged the moment of the baby, she became sorrowful. She wondered if she had the capacity to love and nurture the baby as she should. The fire of resentment was a blazing inferno. As the comparison burst in her mind, so did the song Chariots of Fire. It's a song she loved. The Brooklyn Divas had choreographed and danced to it at school. How ironic she can love a song but not a baby. What if she could love the baby? Would she be strong enough since Ogwin didn't want to be tied with a child now. She was afraid. She just could not face her parents and see the disappointment, hurt and pain. Undoubtedly, they would be angry, and who could blame them? She was only 16. She betrayed their trust. She wouldn't miss. Niecy, her baby sister, who looked up to her. She would miss John and Yvonne too, and she cried for her siblings. And if she didn't see the future before, she did know.

She was cut off from everything and everyone that was familiar to her. Mother, father, sister, brother. Grandmother and her friends. She cried for what she lost and the long, lonely road ahead. What did she do? As the tears tremble on her lashes, she heard the announcement of the conductor from Amtrak. She hesitated on the platform. It was an irrevocable step, and she pulled her case inside. The tears ran unchecked as the train left Penn Station.

Chapter 4

When she got to Mount Vernon, she took a cab to Econo Lodge where she had a reservation. The cabbie was very accommodating, and she stopped and got food. She got brown rice, vegetables with roast pork and chicken. She got mint tea as well. She checked in without problem. Her worldly air or the sleepy attendant didn't ask for ID or three credit cards might have helped too. The hotel wasn't posh, but it was decent. The linen was clean. So was the bathroom. She did not see any critters. She had an appointment with the sisters of Mercy at 2.30 pm and she had ample time to change her appearance. She had a wig, dark glasses, heavy mascara, bold lipstick and sandals laced to her calf. She needed to look older than her 16 years. Her reason was to disguise her identity in case she ran into someone she knew. Once she was armored, she set out to walk. After 10 minutes of walking, she hailed a cab. When she got there, she spoke with Sister Katherine O'Connor, went through the intake process building on what she had told Father Vincent Dalio when she sought his help. It was a home for unwed mothers. She did not want to stay behind bars this weekend and they sprayed enough agitation that it was suggested to think it over and return Monday. However, she asked to tour the facility to calm her misgiving and would help her make the appropriate decision. She was introduced to Sister Petrona and Sister Grace.

The place was serviceable. There were units of eight- four bedrooms equipped with single beds, two windows with a chest of drawers between them, a closet and two chairs. It was a big area that served as a kitchen, dining and sitting room. There was a full-size refrigerator and stove as well as two showers, two toilets and two basins. She appreciated the windows and the lights it offered. She believed she could be comfortable, but she needed to let it get familiar in her head. She calculated she'd be there roughly three to four months but would not tell anyone that. The adoption process could come later. She moved in the following Monday July 16th. All things being equal, she should give birth early September by her guess. She just guessed because she was too afraid to go prenatal care, despite the number of Satellite clinics Kings County Hospital has.

Martha moved in with seven other girls. They were friendly enough and her roommate was Sasha. She seemed a little reserved, though she smiled and said welcome. As on her tour, the place was clean. Funny, she just noticed built-in shelves over one wall. Books were on it. There was a new single sheet set on her bed with a pillow. Martha vowed to personalize her space as quickly as possible. The residents had dinner together except for special occasions. Thanksgiving, Christmas, etcetera. Sasha wasn't very talkative, but she smiled a lot. Martha sensed deep and the eyes were shadowed. One thing for sure, they all have stories. She likes Sasha. She seemed like a gentle soul. Soon she became friends with her roommate. Sasha was highly intelligent, more so than the others or so it seemed. She was from the Bronx and attended Bronx High School for Science. She wanted to be a forensic scientist. She seemed versed in bio and chemistry, statistics, mathematics, physics, calculus. She had awards for science for mathematics. So, what is she doing there? Two weeks later, Martha found out she was friends with Langs Woodburn. They were friends through high school. She got pregnant on Prom night. He's gone off to Harvard and she is pregnant and has to abandon going to Syracuse University to complete her study. He suggested an abortion and when she said no, he said she was on her own. He gave her cash and when she refused, he bought a money order and mailed it to her. She still had it. Her parents hit the roof when they found out. She went to stay with her grandmother for a while, but tension grew between her parents. And her grandmother. Her grandmother wanted to help her, but she found out about Sister of Mercy and ran. She was in touch with her grandmother and talked almost every day. She gave her tips about her pregnancy and promised to be there at her delivery. Her father disowned her. Her mother, who gives in to her father, cannot talk to her openly. She calls her every week. If her father picks up, she hangs the phone up or speaks in pig Latin then he hangs up.

Martha considered her situation. At least Sasha had the courage to tell her parents. She tucked tail and ran. Her father would not forgive her. Maybe her mother would eventually forgive her, but she may never know. She cried herself to sleep that night. She missed her mother. She needed her mother. She just couldn't go home. She called earlier, as usual, just to hear her mother's voice. She called several times since her flight from home and talked with Jonathan, Yvonne and Denise when she was sure her parents were not at home. They wanted to know where she was and when she said she was. Coming home. She promised them one day, but not anytime soon. She asked about her mother. Poor mom, tired and worked so hard to appease her paternal grandmother. She believed her father should have married a doctor. A barbie doll called Greta. Paternal grandmother Gertrude never grew tired of mentioning Greta and that her father was a brilliant lawyer at Schuster and Gilman. Martha regretted her actions more as she knew Grandma Gertrude would find some way to blame her mother. She wondered how Grandfather married Gertrude. Did she use a rolling pin on him like Prissy to snag Leghorn/ Grandpa

Wes like the cartoon, she thought maliciously. Grandpa Wes had to be a victim.

She realized her irresponsible behavior had wide rippling effects. Poor mom, she thought. Her grandmother can be snobbish at best and vitriolic at worst. She loved Calvin. He was a spitting image of Dad as was Yvonne, and Denise who looked like the Chimes. (She was a cross between both parents and looked like maternal grandmother). So those were Grandmother Gertrude's favorites. She was Grandmother Ethlyn's favorite. Unlike Gertrude, Grandma Ethlyn loved and got along with her dad. She accepted who mom married for who he is, he understood there was. She understood there was fragile peace between the families. So would be wise not to incur any more friction. What was the saying? What a tangled web we weave when first we practice to deceive. She thought morosely, if regret was currency, then she'd be a millionaire. Right now, she had loads of regret. She was sorry for lying to her mother, she was not sexually active when she was. That deception cost her, her family. She missed Denise and Yvonne so much. Even when she went out with Ogwin, she never neglected them. She was always the big sister, helping with schoolwork, braiding their hair and treating them at McDonald's or Burger King. She even suffered through cartoon movies she had no interest in, although not so much this last year.

She tried to settle in the routine of the house and three weeks after she got there had a clinical appointment. She went because she had no prenatal care. Now, she was firm in her decision that she would give the baby up for adoption and with the aborted abortion, she needed care. They could more accurately predict the due date for the baby. She saw Dr. Gruniche. When he asked how advanced her pregnancy was, she said she was unsure. He didn't think it was a problem. He examined her and asked who the OBGYN. She confessed she had no prenatal care. He was surprised. Then he seemed elated. He called to the nurse, Miss Moss to discuss her confinement. She marveled at the antiquated word and lost interest in his conversation with the nurse. They both seemed really excited. When she asked if something was wrong, she was assured she was fine. Martha thought they were behaving oddly, as if they had got a treat. She was not reprimanded or berated. She didn't know then what they discovered.

Both she and Sasha became very good friends. She could speak with her about college, or career aspirations. Sasha really knew her stuff and Martha encouraged her to seek delay in accepting her scholarship. Martha thought she was too brilliant to give up the opportunity without a fight. With a 4.0 average, she urged her to fight for the scholarship. Her fight became her fight and the bonding was cemented. Notwithstanding, she missed Barbara. Steph and Sophia, but Sasha was the best antidote for that. Besides, the fight caused her to focus on someone else other than herself. Sasha was keeping her baby. Martha felt a heavy dose of guilt. Quiet Sasha has more courage than I do, she mused. Despite being disowned by her parents, she wanted her baby. She said she lost her parents and, love of her life so she can grieve one time. She is staying a year at Mercy, then lets the baby stay with her grandmother; her maternal grandmother, that is. They discussed it. She would have bonded with the baby by then. She wanted the baby to know her very well to know his mother. Of that she was certain. She would not leave but called it periodic separation.

Martha wished she had it together like her new friend Sasha. The others in the house noticed how well they got along. Sasha had told her she had little in common with them except for premature pregnancy. They talked about boys all the time, the latest fashion shoes, dresses, sneakers, about Sephora, Kate Spade, Michael Kors. She wanted to keep learning, doing organic chemistry through an online course. She said she was on a detour to her career and her destination was around the bend, so she didn't have time to talk garbage. Those designers did what they needed to do to succeed. The house comprised of two Hispanics, 15 years old, three Caucasians and three Afro Americans. Cultural identity was not a thing, but it wouldn't be possible without an even number of teens. That is why cooking was such a contentious affair. There was such an upheaval in the type of food cooked at times. She likes spaghetti and meatballs but, spaghetti with sauce without meat. No. They reached a compromise, spaghetti and meatballs only.

As she finished her first month there, she got more and more acclimatized to her new life. There were rules and curfew, which didn't bother her half as much as the separation from the family in Brooklyn. She missed her little sisters terribly. She called many times, hung up if Denise didn't pick up. She was lucky that on occasion she got to speak with all of them; Denise, Yvonne and Calvin. She was elated when she spoke with them and held onto the contact. It was her lifeline. She called her grandmother Ethlyn weekly. It was rather stilted at first, but once her grandmother accepted, she was not going to disclose her whereabouts, gave up asking. She asked Marty (her grandmother's pet name for her) if she was in trouble, and if she is doing okay, is she taking care of herself, eating properly, seeing the doctor? One day she asked Marty if the flight from Brooklyn had to do with that slick-looking boy with the car. She prevaricated.

"Well, yes and no. I am not seeing him anymore and he doesn't know where I am and that's the way I like it." She made the sign of the cross although she wasn't Catholic. She hated lying to her grandmother, but she could not compromise her by telling the real reason she left home. It would cause a rift between her and her daughter, her mother. Even when Nana asked bluntly.

"Are you pregnant?" Her heart skipped a beat.

She prevaricated again. "What makes you think that?" she hedged.

"Maybe that headlong flight out of Brooklyn. Remember Marty, it is something that is coming. Babies grow, my granddaughter. It would show sooner or later. So, you will mess up. Wish to Jesus you didn't, but it's not the end of the world. Call your mother. She's desperately sick worrying about you. Oh Marty, Marty."

"I got to go, Grandma," she said choked.

She cried in her pillow that night again. Why didn't she just admit it to her parents and grandmother and get through the berating, anger and recrimination. What's with this obsession with secrecy. Look at the load of torment she is going through. She should be joyful. She can conceive, even if outside wedlock and she looked like a Goodyear blimp. Against her desire, she gained twenty pounds. Thanks to her 5-foot 8 frame, it could've been worse. She thanked the gods for delaying the growth of the baby. One day it was a mound and next the Goodyear blimp. Looking like that, she has no desire to be on the street to be seen by anyone she may know. Furthermore, it is too hot, and she suffers from fatigue.

She has started to bond with the other girls in the unit other than Sasha. They are the perfect ebony and ivory pair. If there is a big positive, it is meeting Sasha Steadman. She is sweet and kind, not loud or boisterous but she gets her point across. She's very pretty and her face lights up when she smiles. She's academically gifted. Maritza Osmo and Isabella Toledo are roommates; Bethanne Lynne and Melissa Greenspan and Shaquana Deare and Keisha Burns are the last pair. Melissa and Isabella are barely 15 years. Both have birthdays in October and November. So technically they are 14 years. Both are from opposite backgrounds. Maribel (Maritza's mother) works in a factory and develops a drug habit after she became friends with Luis. Her father went back to Puerto Rico, while mom Maribel worked. After she met Luis, he and his friends Pedro and Julio started visiting. Luis, spent more and more time there and invited all those guys who wore flashy clothes, drank a lot and did drugs.

One day Peter came by and said Luis asked him to pick up a package. She let him in and that's when he touched her breast. And it progressed from there to kisses, still more touching then sex. And nine months later, she was pregnant, and her mother put her out. Her father said not to send her to Puerto Rico and Mom should deal with the mess she created with her drug dealer buddies. So, her mother found out about the home for unwed mothers.

Marty cringed when she heard. That is statutory rape. She asked Maritza if her mother had called the police or reported it. Mommy's getting money from Luis, so he said his buddy can't go to jail and Maritza wanted it. She never cried out or told her mother. Her mother turned on her and blamed her. At that point she started to cry. Maritza said there was no one to help. The whole family called her a tramp and good for nothing. Said she tried to talk with her mother, but she was always high on crack. She always brushed her off, saying later. Eventually she stopped working, but by then it was too late. Pedro would cover her when she started to scream. He forced himself on her even though she asked him, then begged him to stop. She hugged the Maritza telling her how sorry she was for her pain and it was not her fault. Martha thought you predator; someone will stop you one day. My goodness: 14 years old and you think it's okay to have sex with a minor? You a grown as man of 26? Oh man, and she thought she had it bad. The poor thing was raped. You know, a 14-year-old cannot give consent. It would have been horrible even if the boy was a teenager but a grown 'ass' man. And silently she vowed she would stop the predators one day. One at a time!

Isabella's mother was an LPN, divorced from her father and she lived with this man. She and in wisdom worked nights and left this man with her fully developed 14-year-old daughter. So, he started coming into her room at nights to check if she was sleeping. He ran his hand over her saying he was checking if it was a person or pillows or she was out with her friends at night. His hands would linger on her bottom. She started to lie on her stomach because of his nightly checks. She asked him not to come to her room. Some nights when he opened the door and she'd move so he didn't have to come in and touch her. He stopped for a while until her friend Earl visited one day, and he saw him whispering to her and she was giggling. They shared an earphone, and Earl had his arms around her waist. They were rocking together, and he ordered Earl out. She told him to mind his own business. Her mother was at the hairdresser. After that he told her mother that he was watching out for her.

He started locking her in her room and, while asleep, would come in. He used to kiss and fondle her jeering her they were alone. Her mother trusted him, and she wouldn't believe anything she said. He was right. Mother didn't believe his advances. I got tired of fighting him and sex became regular, like once a week. Then he wanted to pick me up from school when I wanted to hang out with my friends. Worst, if that friend was a boy, he'd order me to get in the car. So, after one such incident, he took my curling iron, and I told mom. What he was doing as he was watching me. He was slick telling her he saw a boy kissing me and as punishment he took the curling iron. After that I asked him if he felt like a hero, sleeping with mother and daughter. He said he liked fresh, tender meat. And that's me. He was lucky to get two for the price of one. That's when I realized what I allowed to happen. I told my guidance counselor who told the principal who called the State Central Registry – aka BCW. A case worker came and removed me from the home. When I did medical clearance at Bellevue, I was found to be pregnant. Yes, the fox was left to guard the chicken; so, I asked not to be home, and the law guardian told the family court judge, and I asked to be far away from Brooklyn. So, this is where I was placed. She too was crying, and Martha wondered at the wisdom of placing these two young victims together as roommates as she hugged her. She realized the fashion craze was possibly to hide their pain. And they are just 14 years old, normal stuff! Who consoled them? Suddenly she felt much older and wiser. Yes, there is a bunch of dirty old men who preyed on the innocent and naive. Melissa and Bethanne both have boyfriends that have sudden attacks of amnesia and are not the fathers of these babies. These confessions are cathartic, and the eight girls bonded even the 14-year-olds.

From that day we became a family, and we looked out for each other. The youngsters began to make plans to return to school. They are waiting to be placed in a mother child program. They will keep their babies, and their foster mother will care for the baby while the girls are in school, but when home that responsibility changes and becomes theirs. However, a pact was formed that they would always maintain contact. Each person should contact even one other person weekly, so no one would ever be alone. Martha felt guilty during the bonding. The confession never revealed her true name. Although it seemed lopsided, she was not insincere to always remain in touch and one day started a group like MADD. She went to the library and spoke with the librarian who told her about MADD and she read all about the organization. Somewhere in the back of her mind she vowed to stop the predators. She indicated this purpose to Sasha, who was interested, but said they'd have to be pregnant free and situated. She believed that Isabella (Issi) and Maritza (Ritza) are too young but must be encouraged to complete their high school, get their diplomas and go to college. The other four girls are 16 or 17 and 18 years old.

As Marty listened to Sasha, Melissa, Isabelle, Shaquana talked positive about the child each is carrying, she wondered if she is abnormal. She does want to become a mother, but fear and anger and guilt dodges her every thought, and footsteps. The what ifs are enemies. One day she went to the park two blocks away in her disguise: flaming wig, dark glasses, nose ring. She has to talk to/with the baby. She found a tree away from the screaming children and those playing ball. She hears the shrieks of delight, the laughter, and see the happy faces. She watched as some tumble, pick themselves up and rush off before mother's or babysitters can get to them. There is pride on the faces of some adults, and indulgent smiles. And she smiles at the picture. And she feels that tug again at her heart. Is she doing the right thing? What will become of her? Like her Nana says it's not the end of the world. Is she really putting pride above her unborn child? Is she rejecting the child just to save face? The marks of pregnancy, of giving birth is indelible. It will always be there.

So, in a monologue she tells the baby she is afraid and does not want to make a mistake that would ruin her (the baby's) life any further. She is sorry for the abortion attempt, but his father does not want to be a dad, and she is terrified of doing it on her own. She asked for forgiveness. She prayed that she would have the courage to keep the baby. She is deeply conflicted. She tried to explain the panic she feels each time she sees them alone in the future. That she does love her, but the recurring dream she has, her body is drenched with sweat, and she is hyperventilating. She asks her unborn baby to forgive her. She cried and cried and was only aware she was crying when someone asked if she was okay and can they get her some water? She wiped her eyes and told them she was okay. Marty left the park with the others. She bought apple, orange and cranberry juice. It was hard work toting the juice home, especially as it was the gallon containers.

Each girl is officially given her EDC – (expected due date). The EDC dates are close to each other. Lamaze classes are conducted through VNS. Each girl is partnered with another. Isabella and Maritza are encouraged to partner with an older girl. This made their situation real and imminent. It underlined the seriousness of their positions and symbolic crossing over into pseudo motherhood - a leaving behind of childhood and innocence. These steps cannot be retraced to innocence and wonder. Some man took care of that. Some creep took two 14-year-old girls with callous disregard for their innocence and future. No matter if they are big for their ages, whether they have a bustline, that is 32 or 42. They are in need of protection; the creeps get away with it. The problem is pervasive across ethnic groups, languages and color. Marty knew then a multicultural approach is needed to bridge the divide. She is convinced that cultural stereotypes and prejudice must be bridged, and all these groups banding together like MADD could effect a change. Dr. M. King did that before he was assassinated, before she was even conceived. Rev Jesse J has the Rainbow Coalition with a very political agenda mixed with social justice, but it didn't address young girls plight and dilemma in particular and young boys in general.

Chapter 5

During periods of lax, she thought of the mother, a nurse, who left her 14-year-old daughter in the house with a man she was not married to and not the child's father. Many parents work two jobs so they can 'make' it, but at what cost? Nothing is wrong with working two jobs but is the payoff worth it. And here comes the predator, just waiting for the vulnerable children to pounce on them. The worst part is many are relatives and family friends. Everything is wrong with that level of deception. She prayed that she'd never sit on a jury with one such as these. He would not get away. Family Court was too tame. The DAs should pick up the case after it's indicated but an overworked court system let the perps free or keep going like a revolving door. Repercussions are not severe enough. She wanted ten minutes with a perp. Just ten minutes and he'd be cured from having sex with 12-year-olds and the like. It was unfortunate there was no such provision or allowance made in the law. But she believes where there is a will there's a way. Her passion was to do something. If she can save one12 or 13-year-old child from the clutches of one predator, whatever risk is involved is worth it. And the germ of an idea was born. It needed militant, even radical belief for the greater good. However risking leg or limb and offspring is not required. Security of self is a must. They'd undertake operations, hit hard and fast and depart. There's total anonymity. There is a pact among the friends, but their stage working name is Women Against Sexual Predators- WASP. There's another organization with similar acronym but, it's neither legislative nor owned. She'd do what she could until she could fully get the other ladies on board.

There is a tremendous level of responsibility that is needed. She does not want to swap one exploited situation for another. This must be free will. No one is to be coerced, shamed, burdened with guilt to commit to WASP. She will do her research. Computers are fantastic but whatever is done must look like it's research for term a paper. She knew how to get information from the librarian and thus cover her research. Furthermore, if she's to have things organized for the next five years, preparation must start now. She prayed, though not consciously, that her plan will resonate with even four of the friends, so it's critical everyone keeps in touch.

By the time her EDC five of the other girls had delivered. They knew separation was imminent, but with each armed with phone numbers believed they'd never been out of touch. The day she delivered was a horrifying day. September 7th. She was scared. When her water broke, she was in the yard, sweeping the back patio. The puddle of water by her feet was the first clue. She had grown accustomed to the pain across her back and usually engaged in activities to distract herself. She called Sasha and Sister Grace. Sister Grace and Sasha called the hospital- Westchester General and Dr. Gruniche. She forgot everything from the lamaze class except the throbbing in her back and stomach. She let out a scream and Sister Grace jumped. Doctor Gruniche was not at the hospital when they got there. Sister Grace was able to give all pertinent information and, because they were registered everyone knew the girls are from Catholic Charity Sisters of Mercy, she believed eased the way. A message came that Dr. Gruniche said to go through her lamaze routine and hold the delivery.

She screamed, "I can't hold anything," and another contraction hit. "What is he doing? she wailed. They said he turned and was in" and what else was said was lost in midair. She was sweating and was hastily taken to the delivery room. Sasha tried to talk her through. "Pant baby pant. Easy, honey. Just couple more minutes. Hold my hand."

"Get her in position, said the Nurse Practitioner. Get any doctor. What the heck? Hold it." The NP addresses her, don't push until I tell you. Bear down when I tell you. You are doing fine. Ok honey."

And she cried. And she longed for her mother. She longed for Nana. Oh, I'm so sorry Mama, so sorry. And Sasha held her while the NP coaxed and, then Dr. Gruniche appeared. She delivered and while he held the baby, her blood pressure started to fall. They worked to get the placenta out. She heard there is another one. She's bleeding heavy and now in semi-daze and the Doctor shooed them out telling them to take the girl, the baby girl. He and his nurse remained. She believed she saw something jumping up and heard a baby cry, and she lost consciousness. She came awake to hear complication after delivery. She struggled to talk or to get up, but sank in oblivion. The second time she woke Sasha was there.

Her friend kissed her cheeks. "Thank God you are okay. Oh, my I was never so frightened. You gave everyone a scare."

She tried to piece things together. She demanded to see her baby girl, that the bassinet be brought. She fought with the nurses and demanded to know details of what happened in the delivery room. She was told there is only one baby. She insisted there was a second baby. She heard that baby cry. They tried to tell her otherwise, but she knew what she heard. Finally, Dr. Greenwich admitted there was a boy that was still born. Marty insisted. The dead doesn't cry. That baby cried. In the end, Dr. Gruniche shows papers- Baby boy Brett. She asked for a copy of the footprint whether alive or dead, she also wanted to see the baby. They gave her medicine to calm her, showing her a lifeless body, but maternal instinct kicked in. "That is not my baby. He is alive," she said.

On the third day, when the baby was to be discharged and processed, she insisted that Doctor Gruniche not be there. She demanded to speak with the adoptive parents alone or the adoption stops. The parties would wear masks. In the brief five minutes meeting, Marty committed to memory hair, eyes, dress, mannerism, hands and voice. She told the parents it made her feel less like she's giving away her baby; that her little girl is with family. She named the little girl Sarai. The name was no accident; its Hebrew alternative was Sarah. Since Martha Renee Chimes did not give birth, rather Novelette Masters did, she needs some way to identify her daughter. She remembered someone say what's in a name. That pull on her innards, made it mandatory Baby Master has a name. She also named the alleged still born, Ethan Gabriel Masters. She accepted what a horrible mess she was in. Deceit has a high price and an exacting task master. How can she continue. How can she possibly explain to the others her true name after that great bonding experience?

She rationalized she couldn't possibly reveal who she is now because she'd have nowhere to go. She needs shelter and needs to hide until she can make herself known to her family. She made sure to keep in touch with her siblings and grandmother. So, her parents wouldn't continue to pursue a missing person's report; nor be tempted to get a PINS (person in need of supervision). That, she was sure, ended when the child turns 16 plus, she hoped pride would keep them from doing the PINS. She knows to the police she was just another rebellious teenager- runaway and they'd take the report but, wouldn't waste time looking for her. She hoped they wouldn't change their mode of operation now and start searching for her. But with her permanently covered head and tinted contact lens felt safe from the police.

Marty was listless. She agreed to give one child up for adoption, not two. If she had known, then she would make it a condition, that both be placed together. The full weight of what she had done fell on her and she could not get out of bed. She was numb. She did not understand. She balked at the idea of one child, but why is she so upset there's another baby taken from her? And her deep desire to know him. She refused food and the social worker was sent to talk with her. Miss Jordan Andreesuis, the social worker, asked about her well-being, and if there was a particular food or dish she would like. She shook her head. She wanted to know what was on her mind and if there's someone she wanted to contact. What can she do to help her? Was she having second thoughts about the adoption and, did she get counseling prior to? Marty looked at her and shook her head.

"Am I one of your patients?" Marty asked.

Social worker Jordan frowned. "Why? That's not exactly what I thought you'd want to talk about."

"I just wondered, seems like you are in a rush," said Marty.

"I'm sorry, I don't understand. I'm here because I believe you have remorse about the adoption. I want to help you with this transition There are support groups for women who feel guilty for giving up their child for adoption."

"Well, social worker, how long since you came to my room?" asked Marthy.

"I've been here almost ten minutes," she said.

Marty interjected. "Yet you have looked at your watch five times. Since you cannot spare the time let me make it easy; you can go-wouldn't want to detain you. Thanks for stopping by," she said sweetly and closed her eyes, but not before she saw shock and cheeks flushed with embarrassment. The social worker tried to engage her after that, spluttering a denial and an apology but she turned her back and pulled the sheet over her head. She blocked everything she said after that until she left five minutes later. She can stick the token visit where the sun doesn't shine. Let her go fabricate notes now about her visit.

Nurse Radcliffe comes in.

"What's up girl? Why is Jordan's cheeks flaming? What did you do to her? Come on, spill your Spitfire."

Marty liked Nurse Radcliffe. They hit it all from the moment they met.

"I didn't do nothing; I just put her out of her misery of visiting me. Tell me, hypothetically, if someone keeps looking at his watch, what do you think is happening?"

"Well, maybe it's habit, discomfort, or they are on a schedule and checking to manage their time, or maybe busy and have to be somewhere else," said Nurse Radcliffe.

"I prefer the last one, busy and has some place else to be. She came in and in ten minutes- her estimate of time and she looked at her watch five times. Really? Don't do me any favors. So, I told her she did her duty. She stopped by and she could go, didn't want to detain her."

Marty saw nurse Radcliffe's grin as she struggled to be serious.

"Oh no Masters! You shouldn't have done that."

"Too late, I already did. She has some place to be then she should go. What is it? A piece rate system?"

"Now what are you talking about?" the nurse asks in exasperation.

Marty was unrepentant. "You know, get paid by the number of patients you see. Don't want to deprive her of her livelihood. Token visit; Token and talk? Or is this special treatment for us?"

Nurse Radcliffe looks stern. "What do you mean treatment for us?"

"Us teenagers," said Marty.

"Oh okay! I don't think so though. Every patient matters. Young, old and in between. We offer care across the board."

"If you say so," Marty grumbled. She shuttered her face after that.

"Do you know you are the typical teenager? Moody, blow, hot and cold. I must say it's the most alert I've seen since yesterday. Sassy is not a good thing, but now I know there's a real person inside there. You were so dejected and listless now a little light is in your eyes. Whatever causes that spark, I am glad. But honey, you do need to see somebody. You have the beginning of what could be postpartum depression. Maybe our on-staff psychiatrist can talk with you."

"Me and the shrink! Nurse Radcliffe, I know you mean well, but no, I'm good. It will pass. There is no help with what ails me. No one can help me."

Don't say that! That's a defeatist attitude. Everyone can be helped, if you don't sink in despair and wallow in what might have been. Don't go down that road. It's a slippery slope. You are young, bright, beautiful. There's so much expectation for you. See, I'm rooting for you. This is just a detour, honey. Keep going. You are so much more than you think. You can do anything. Tell the universe how great you are, that you are here to conquer and direct and to do a bunch of good. Masters, you are a champion! Champions don't quit. No, the brave never quit. Work on you. Believe in you and forgive yourself. Give yourself permission to be happy. No one has the right to judge you, whatever it is. God forgives sins. He will forgive you. Ask Him and then move on. You know, Maya Angelo says, "Let gratitude be the pillow you pray on at night." Don't let having a baby derail your dreams. There's a big whole world and God is in it. And if you seek Him, you will find Him.

Nurse Radcliffe did not know where that speech came from. She had not planned it, but there was a compulsion to speak faith and belief in this young woman. She feels she bonded with this teenager more than any other. She tugged at her heart. It was all she could do from crushing her against her breast.

Marty was taken aback by the vehement speech by Nurse Radcliffe. That was powerful. Can she crawl out of the hole she stepped in? The lie, the deceit to the parents, siblings and to her grandparents. She has been fighting despair since she found out she was pregnant. Now there is no baby or rather, are no babies. Would Nurse Radcliffe help her? Would she understand she needed to find her son? Would she believe that she heard the baby cry? That he could not have been stillborn, that Dr. Gruniche lied. That he cannot be trusted! She remembered how happy he was the first time she saw him. He seemed excited, saying this is good. No scolding, no scathing remark for not having prenatal care. That Rat knew she was having twins but didn't tell her. She longed to confront him. She had refused to see him, but maybe she should ask to see him. And make another go at it. But this would be another step in deception because she needed to appear depressed so she could stay longer than three days to see what she would uncover about the good doctor.

Marty was grateful. For the speech, she was still running a low-grade fever and hoped it was enough to give her an extra day in the hospital. Not eating can work in our plans? If she is weak then they'd have to keep her. She hoped they would. They wouldn't force her to eat. She liked milkshakes but hoped her diet wasn't milk only. That's for babies! At the thought she felt a stab in her stomach. She clutched her stomach. She hoped the bleeding had stopped or slowed really. Where did the hospital get Dumbo Ears for the monthlies. Disney World! These are antique straight out of the 30s. somewhere. She didn't really care. Even to a novice like herself tampons are a no- no. She'd ask Sasha to bring Always. She shuddered- elephant ears.

Chapter 6

The social worker came back, much to her surprise. Maybe Nurse Radcliffe talked to her because she came without her watch. She apologized and said they'd start over. She agreed to meet her halfway and had a productive meeting. One thing she said that resonated with her was the intimacy she shared with her baby and that she nurtured the baby until birth. And lack of continuity can make you feel sad, but there are support groups to help you and to come to terms with their decision. That feeling of guilt or remorse is normal. She was paged after twenty minutes and promised to return.

Nurse Radcliffe came to do her vitals. She knew she didn't have to, but she came. She declared the temperature was still a little high, would ask the doctor to see her and prescribe something for her.

"Well, what about Tylenol? Isn't that the preferred drug? Drugs allegedly without repercussions," she said cheekily.

Nurse Radcliffe rolled her eyes then asked how the session went with the social worker. She told her very well and social worker Andreesius; she was not wearing her watch. Nurse Radcliffe laughed.

"Okay, I'm happy the meeting went well."

"Do you have children, Nurse Radcliffe?"

"Why?"

"Just curious. You seem to care. Thank you for encouraging me."

"Well, I have a son and daughter. His name is Justin."

"Oh, that's nice. How old is he? Does he play sports? What about your daughter?"

"My daughter is 12 going on 36, apple her father's eyes to the chagrin of her mother. A real Diva and Daddy's girl. She is Sheika Gian. He is 14 and he loves basketball. He has ambition to play for the Knicks. He hopes to do what the Knicks has not done in a long time, win a championship, Nurse Radcliffe said with a laugh. Even though he loves Steph Curry and LeBron, he wants to be the sparks on the Knicks team that John Starks was and block like Patrick Ewing."

"Aren't those old players? Even I don't know them."

"Well, my dear, in the days when I watched basketball, the Knicks were bad. I mean bad! You had Oakley, Buck Williams, Anthony Mason, Hubert Davis, Derek Harper, Greg Anthony, Doc Rivers, Charlie Ward and some others. Those nights when the game was on, don't call, don't come over. That was date night! I took every jump shot with Starks and Davis. Those guys could dish."

"I can see you don't like baseball," Marty said with a smile.

"I loved the game then, but as they retired, I couldn't identify with the team anymore. Do you know I loved Magic Johnson? I learned about Bill Russell though he was ahead of my time. But I learned about Doctor J and the Ruckers tournament and it was after I saw an interview with Doctor Jr, understood where the others learned hang "time. That's in my humble opinion."

That's why that's before my time," she said.

"What are you talking about? You need to watch some old reels on the whole MJ elevate. Never see a poster with Michael Jordan feet off the ground flying to the net. I believe all the players learned that from us New Yorkers. That's where the Ruckus tournament came out of. Don't tell anyone, I said. New York, teach MJ to fly. Just hometown pride and Doctor Julius Erving aka Doctor J was, in my estimation, the first flying

NBA player. Oh, well. Just getting back in it for Justin's sake. He is in the Manifold Club, and they specialize in basketball, so I'm all over Mount Vernon. Bronx, MSG taking and attending games."

"Does his father not take him," Marty asked.

"Oh, Steve. Once in a while. He is a little too enthusiastic so the coaches prefer him not to attend except at MSG where he is not close to the players," she said with a laugh.

She smiled. For a minute, she forgot her problems. She longed to ask for help. It seemed like a great opportunity to ask now.

"Nurse Radcliffe, do you think I'm crazy?" she added softly.

"Of course, not honey. Did someone say you are?"

"Not exactly. You see, my delivery was rough; was hemorrhaging, blood pressure dropped, etcetera. But I know I delivered twins. The doctor said no but I insisted. But even through the pain and blurred vision, I heard. The baby cried. Later, he said the baby was still born."

By this, tears are running unchecked down her cheeks. Hot, scalding tears of anger and despair.

"What? Nurse Madison said and hugged her. Oh my gosh no. Oh Lord no. I'm so sorry honey."

Marthy accepted the comfort but said, "Still born babies don't cry! They showed me a stillborn, but my mother's instinct said he was not mine. I swear he is alive. The Doctor and his Nurse Gretchen lied. That still born baby is not mine."

"Yes, I did read it in the charts. I don't know what to say or do."

"Can you help me find my baby? See who delivered same day or day before I did. I believe they swapped/ stole and sold my baby. I was not hallucinating."

"Those are serious allegations. Masters didn't you know you were having twins?"

"No, she croaked. Up to the time she reached Sisters of Mercy I had no prenatal care. Dr. Gruniche works with them, to take care of us. I was roughly six months before care began. I remember how excited he was. He didn't scold me that I'd had no prenatal care but, saying this is good this is good. He warned me to keep future appointments, prescribed vitamins and folic acid and said everything looked good. The following month I had a sonogram but I'm not sure what I saw. The picture was too grainy, and while printing it said the paper jammed. That is why he was so excited. He had plans for my baby."

"I will see what I can find out," she promised. She squeezed her shoulders and left.

Marty felt better knowing she was trying to find Ethan Gabriel- Baby Brett indeed! Her heart and womb knew her child was alive somewhere. She had doubted her capacity to love, that she would not be an adequate mother so, what is this feeling. What is this desire to find her baby boy. She is giving up his sister so what does it matter? She couldn't explain it, but she wanted him back. Would she still have decided to go forward with the adoption if she knew she was having twins. Someone took that choice away. She wished she could withdraw the consent for adoption. Would the twins know there are two of them. People speak of an irrevocable bond between twins and she wished it was so. She prayed that by some miracle would find each other. Lord Jesus if you are real and the loving God with-hold the sins of their parents. Let it not visit the children. Please God protect my babies.

And this time she curled in a fetal position and cried for her children, the separation, the colossal error she made for the choice she made for the choice she made to deceive. It seemed so simple now. She could've gone to Nana Ethlyn. She would have helped. Now look at this mess. So instead of losing one child she's losing two children. She is tormented over the loss of Gabriel.

After her catheter was removed her temperature spiked, which gave her two additional days in the hospital with the hope nurse Radcliffe would uncover something. Nurse Radcliffe didn't uncover very much. The delivery team remember Doctor Gruniche examining the little girl and handing her over and later when her blood pressure dipped shooed them to take care of the baby and he would take care of the mother. One person remembers seeing a baby and hearing the doctor say. Hiding were you little fella. Believed she heard the baby cry and doctor said respiratory distress to the unfamiliar nurse coming in with a mask, cap and gown and worked on the baby. The doctor said the baby didn't make it. Name him Brett. And the floater nurse wrapped him and took him to the morgue. She said seven women delivered that morning. Nothing seemed out of the ordinary. The other six went home with their babies. So where did this still born baby come from? How did they get her baby out? She posed the question to nurse Radcliffe.

"It's very easy. A gym bag is perfect. You wrap the baby, lower him in and walk out, bag over your shoulder."

"But don't they have cameras and isn't there the wristband that beep if you leave the nursery."

"Yes, but he didn't reach the nursery yet. If they say stillborn then that band wouldn't be activated. You understand that. Oh dear, I wish I found something helpful."

"Yes, you did."

"What?"

"You found that seven women gave birth, including me. If you could give me their demographics I can research when I'm out."

"Master's that's a breach of ethics and hospital policy not to mention HIPPA. I cannot do that."

As her face crumbled, the nurse hugged her. "Please don't cry."

"Why can't you if you say you believe I'm not crazy. Thought you said you trusted my mother's instinct about my son. I'd never agree to adoption if I had known about my son. Please help me. I know I screwed up. Help me to do something right, something unselfish, please," she sobbed.

"My mother's heart ache for you but two wrongs don't make a right."

"No. They lied and cheated. Do not do it for me but an innocent little boy. I'm trying to redeem myself."

Nurse Radcliffe said she'd think about it and let her know. Marty had to be content with that promise. Lying on the bed, remorse gnawed at her. Why didn't she just tell her parents, Nana she was pregnant. Why did she panic? She remembered Isabella and Maritza. They accepted their pregnancy; they would go to a mother and child program but still had the option for adoption. Oh Marty, Marty, you done it this time. She may well be grammatically incorrect if this is where her intellect led her. She was marinating in a sea of deception. She was beguiled by her dream of success and seduced by the glamour of dating an older man. Dating a model! she snorted. Right dating her model. She got caught up with a cad, a narcissist. He was madly in love with himself and his own importance. Why was she stupid enough to believe he could care for her? He and his needs. Resentment towards Ogwin sent the bile to her throat. She inhaled deeply several times to calm herself. As she swallowed, a lump stuck in her throat, and she reached for the cup with water. There was no sense in getting agitated. She had enough on her plate. This was too heavy a load. She will need help to get her through this. She would talk with Sister Grace; she was more approachable.

Chapter 7

On the fifth day in the hospital, Nurse Radcliffe told her that she was limited in what she could do. She gave her the names of the women that delivered. Four lived in Westchester, the other two lived in Mount Vernon. Marty thanked her and when she would've verbalized further Nurse Radcliffe put her fingers to her lips and shook her head. She closed her eyes and clasped her hands and nodded to Nurse Radcliffe.

"I don't know why I helped you, but God forgive me. I have never in my twenty years of nursing violated hip hop. But in my gut, it feels right. Make me proud. Follow your mother's instinct where young Ethan is concerned. And you must pray, even as I will too. Having baby young is not the worst thing that can happen. Don't stop your education. Do well. Do not let one error in judgement define you. The Lord knows I made my fair share of bundles. But my mother was patient and forgiving. There's always forgiveness. All parents are angry, upset, disappointed when their teenage daughter gets pregnant. They have a right to, but this is a brief stop on your journey. Your destination awaits you".

As Marty covered her mouth to stifle a sob Nurse Radcliffe squeezed her shoulder and left quietly. Marty cried for her sins, and she prayed the God of her childhood would again visit her. Why did things go so awry? If she thinks about it anymore, she'll go mad. She longed for her mother's arms. She missed the comfort they usually bring more so Nana.

Through her tears. She packed her belongings. She was still sore and had to walk slowly and gingerly. The doctor said the stitches will disintegrate and should return in two weeks for a follow-up.

Sasha and Sister Grace were there to pick her up. The sisters are not emotionally demonstrative, but Sister hugged her and patted her hand while Sasha was all over her. She had a lot to tell Sasha, especially since she needed her help. The Social workers said the birth certificate would come from the registrar in three to six weeks but only Gabriel's. The original birth certificate for her daughter will eventually be sealed, never to be revealed, while a new one will be issued to the adoptive parents, when everything is finalized. She wished she had asked these questions while she contemplated giving her (Sarai) up for adoption. It's like the pregnancy never happened.

Isn't that what you wanted? her conscience chided. That didn't happen. You wanted it far removed from you. You got what you wanted. Shut the hell up she told her brain. Who asked you? It was then she realized the arduous task ahead. Would she be able to quieten her conscience? Her thoughts? Sasha went in labor 2 weeks later. Two weeks prior, she looked like Pokémon in Macy's Thanksgiving Day Parade. She delivered a baby boy; she named him Gabriel Daniel in honor of her friend's missing baby boy. She was happy for Sasha, but it reinforced she was without her son. She knew it was contradictory, but she could not help how she felt. Was God punishing her? Is that the price of ego? She remembered her mother saying sin is a reproach.

Burdened as she was, she sought Sister Grace. She emptied herself, her soul. She confessed the abortion attempt and the remorse in giving up her daughter, not telling her family about her pregnancy, the pain of making it on her own and the agony of losing her siblings and Nana. She cried and Sister Grace tried to comfort her, telling her to take it easy on herself. She was a child making adult decisions- to try and put it to rest. She made her decision based on her situation. But most of all she must forgive herself. She explained forgiveness. Is an oil that soothes just like the love of Christ. She told her that she should pray and ask God to forgive her. The God who sent his Son to the cross forgives sin, that the last act on the cross was forgiveness. He asked God to forgive those who crucified him as he did, the thief beside him. Spend time in the Chapel, have some alone time with God. He hears and sees all. The great difference is she can go to him, talk to him as a parent, she's to tell him what she cannot tell her parents.

After that, she had several talks with Sister Grace. She saw how Sasha flowered in motherhood, she seemed a natural, bonding with her baby. For the first time, she really looked at the impact of her impetuous actions. She envied Sasha. The enormity of what she had done hit her. It was like a physical blow that she doubled over.

Oh my God what have I done? What did I do? Why didn't she confide in Nana. She had so many opportunities. It was as if Nana knew. She was at the lowest ebb of her life and spent two days in the Chapel. She liked the solace. With a scarf mimicking a mantilla she stayed, and they left her. She just sat, only drinking water. Sister Grace seemed to understand what she was going through and brought a poem to her, understanding her need; that she felt isolated from Christ and his teachings from the Bible and the commandments. The Serenity prayer was more contemporary. The first verse resonated with her, (though she memorized the whole prayer).

God grant me the serenity to accept the things I cannot change. The courage to change the things I can. And the wisdom to know the difference. Thank you, Reinhold Niebuhr, she said. What is your story? One day she would. Look him up. Marty used the first stanza as her mantra. She hung it over her bed. She placed it on a piece of cardboard and used a plastic bag to cover it and cello tape to hold it in place. She attended Gabriel (who became her godson) just like a mother should. She couldn't understand why she was so terrified of having a baby. She wondered if her comfort was knowing that she was not responsible for him full time. Just a couple of hours. Several times during the day, when her thoughts grew dreary and would pull her into a hole, she would repeat the first stanza of the Serenity Prayer. She decided to initiate her search for Gabriel. Caller ID was an issue, but they were able to block it so that it came up private. Thankfully they have the telephone directory, so they called the women posing as Westchester Hospital. They inquired about mother and baby getting information as to the sex of the baby. They got the sex of the babies and the days for well-baby clinic under the guise they were confirming records as well as checking on the well-being of the mother and child. Marty had an interesting conversation with Agnes Dench, one of the mothers. She had a baby boy, Travis Cole. She gushed about the newborn, asking the mother to describe what he looks like now. She asked what she thought of twins and wondered if anyone had twins the day she delivered. She didn't, but there was a lady, Esther, who had a stillborn baby before she got there. She heard the nurses talk about it. Marty empathized with the unfortunate mother and said she hoped she was getting grief counseling. Poor Esther, she commiserated. Hope she is not alone.

"Oh yes. She's Catholic and the priest from Saint Helens was there they said. I believe the nurses found it strange he was there."

Marty said she was glad the priest came and as his parishioner obligated to tend his flock. She apologized for taking up her time and wished her well. She was excited there was a possibility she could find Esther and Saint Helen Catholic Church. That would be the proverbial needle in a haystack. She would have to search Westchester as well as Mount Vernon, but it also meant her baby was alive and Doctor Gruniche was a thief and a liar. She looked at the telephone directory. She would have to search page by page, line by line to find Esther. However, she could find the church and find Esther that way. That is the only chance. Six weeks have passed already. She could hire a Private Eye, but that would expose her. What to do? She was quiet for a few days after the initial excitement of finding out about Esther. How can she possibly prove anything? Maybe she should give up. Oh, Lord, help me, help me forgive the lies and deception, she prayed inwardly.

She saw the shoulders of Sister Grace this time. Sister Grace encouraged her to see Father Vincente Dalio for confession. He wouldn't know who she is as there is a protective screen between the priest and herself. She inhaled and digested this. Today, the Serenity Prayer lost its power. It could not contain her mind today. As she turned to go, she said forcibly to Sister Grace. She was positive Dr. Gruniche stole her baby that there was a stillborn baby before she got there belonged to a lady by the name of Esther. And she believed that's the baby she was shown as her own. Sister Grace's eyes widened in shock.

"What? How do you know this? It's hard to believe, but this is just speculation on your part, isn't it?"

"Maybe, but it follows. She repeated again. When Doctor Gruniche and his nurse examined me, they seemed very excited. When I did the sonogram, it was just a 'blob' with what seemed like bubbles and dark spots. They said the machine was acting up again. When I asked to see the printout the printer jammed, which made it crumple and twisted. I believed them and left. So, you see, Sister Grace, they destroyed the evidence of the sonogram because I didn't have prenatal care and ran from the Bristol clinic. Whatever they knew, they would not know where to find me as I went incognito, as they say," she ended.

"Oh, gracious Redeemer, there must be some other explanation. Dr. Gruniche has worked with us for years and is quite trustworthy," said Sister Grace.

"And I am not?" She asked challengingly.

Oh, no, no, no. This is a shock. I don't mean that. Oh, dear. I have to tell Sister Katherine. This can't be happening! Martha, I am so sorry. I am sorry I wasn't more sensitive to you. The Catholic Church cannot withstand another scandal. I am not suggesting we do nothing or cover this up, but we have to go through the proper channels.

Martha's thoughts stopped. It was something she wanted to forget. Father Davillo and Sister Katherine handled the issue. They found Dr. Gruniche and once confronted, he closed his adoption agency. Nurse Gretchen was found and with the threat of prosecution she said both she and the doctor brokered babies. Martha's baby was alive taken from the hospital in a doctor's bag. The five pound seven ounces baby boy was given to a couple in Connecticut. She did not know all the details. Said the mother had, had several miscarriages and was desperate for a child, any child. The couple believed Dr. Gruniche ran an adoption agency CUAMUS (Latin translated We Care) Dr. Gruniche did everything with this couple. Said they were wealthy and willing to pay very generously to get ahead of the line. He said Novlette was having remorse about giving up the girl, but the boy was a bonus she did not know about. She confessed that Gruniche promised her marriage; that he'd divorce his wife, and they would go away together. But he lied. He used her. She had no record of anything. Sadly, a case like this would look like a jilted lover.

Dr. Gruniche closed his operation. No files were found. Everything was burnt or flushed down the toilet literally. Absolutely no records were found anywhere, and he took off. It was as if he evaporated. He'd turned in his keys to his office in White Plains. He lived in the affluent Scarsdale area. He certainly could afford the luxurious suburb. If he was able to barter babies, have a private practice and work at Westchester General, he was wealthy. Each time it looked like a breakthrough, they suffered a setback. Martha felt a fleeting tinge of sympathy for the jilted Gretchen

Whitmore, and it was gone. She helped steal her son. She seemed naïve not to get some insurance – copy records, take pictures. That is a juvenile move something a teenager would do, not a mature woman. All in the name of love.

Martha rolled her eyes and made a disgusted sound. What can one ten do? How could she find her baby? Would she find her baby? Would going to Connecticut resolve anything. Martha Chime never gave birth, only Novelette Masters. Even the birth certificate would show that, she reasoned; she'd never officially changed her name. Plus, how many celebrities entered hospitals, drug rehab under an assumed name. Not that she is a celebrity, but it could be applied to her. She did not want anyone to know who she was or her whereabouts. That reasoning held for a while. Nurses could attest that she had babies, and she had met with Sarah's adoptive parents. Despite what the birth certificate said after the adoption was complete. She gave birth to her, to them. Sarai had the cutest puckered up face with a big thatch of hair as black as raven's wings soft and downy. She didn't immediately look like her, and she didn't know whether to be thankful or sad.

Martha admitted to the futility of her search for Gabriel. Why wasn't God helping her? Why was he so silent. She went back to the Serenity Prayer. One Saturday, she ventured to Connecticut. She told Sasha what she was doing. She told herself all she had to do was look for an Afro American landscaper for him to afford Dr. Granite's price must be opulent. Then she contacted Gretchen to ask what the couple looked like. The husband was Caucasian and the wife Afro American. Now she understood why Doctor Greenwich had pressed her about the father of her baby. That's why his face lit up like Rockefeller Christmas tree, she thought cynically. He must have been in ecstatic- a free baby to sell without complications. No parental consent, no opposition. She remembered hearing. The song Ebony and Ivory a duet by Michael Jackson and Paul

McCartney, so she dubbed the Connecticut couple E and I, Ebony and ivory. She boosts herself by speaking inwardly to be optimistic. That she must try. Quitting or failing to explore every possibility is not acceptable. So, she took Metro North.

She took off her mask except for dark glasses. She wore beige slacks and navy-blue shirt with purple lipstick and mascara (used beyond the three months recommendation). She was blessed with long lashes and didn't need extension. She brushed her hair back, pulled in a ponytail and formed a bun using Nature edge control for perfection. She was now just another young girl. Yes, she was well dressed. She gained about an inch to her waist and no one looking at her would know that she was pregnant a short time ago. That suited her.

As Metro North sped its way to Connecticut, she watched the countryside. She realized there was no place like New York. She pulled out her crossword puzzle when she saw a man looking at her, she wanted no conversation, polite or otherwise. She averted her eyes. For one, it was too early to pick anyone up. Secondly, she was not a Happy Meal, she thought. She became engrossed in the puzzles for a while, but listened out for Stanford stop. Before long, Martha felt drowsy. She closed her eyes. She took her iPad MP3 player and started to listen to music. She smiled at Usher's Yeah. Then she listened to Jack Just Slide DJ Casper. She went back to Michael's Thriller album. The man can sing. She loved watching the videos of Billie Jean and beat it. For the first time in a long time, she felt like a teenager. She loved Destiny Child and TLC as well. Waterfalls is her favorite by TLC. Listening to the music calmed her churning thoughts as she tried many times without success to sing along. She was not ready. When the train stopped her heart skipped a beat. Might could feel fear creeping in. Her stomach was in knots. And as fear inched its way further, she felt a rushing wind in her ears. She swallowed the lump in her throat or tried to anyway. She had no idea what she would say to the couple. If she found them, she couldn't just say the child you adopted was stolen. She inhaled as she exited the station. She pulled a single sheet of paper from her bag. The first address was Premium Landscaping Inc. 1297 Cedar Grove St. There were taxis on the ramp waiting. But she went back inside to speak with an employee. She wanted to have an idea where she was going. Also, she could show her list so she'd know those that were in close proximity to each other.

Cedar Grove and Maple Street were close to each other, roughly ten blocks apart. She took the taxi to G& F Landscape 989 Maple St. Swallowing her fear, she decided she'd pretend she's seeking employment. That seems like an excellent cover story. Pasting a smile on her lips she entered the store. There were tools of the trade visible along with earthenware pots, plants and pictures of manicured lawns and hedges. Her eyes darted around looking for employees. The pictures pulled her towards them, and as she gazed, a voice said hello. She jumped.

"Oh, I'm sorry. Said an elderly man. I did not mean to startle you. Can I help you young lady?"

For a minute, she didn't answer. Recovering from the fright she shook her head.

"I'm sorry. I am looking for the owner," she said with a half-smile.

"Well, you found him. Wilbert Armstrong at your service. Yes, Sir."

She shook his arm while thinking. He is as old as the hills. He must be the right side of 60. But she said politely,

"Please to meet you. Are you by any chance hiring Sir?"

"Oh, he said. We do a fair amount of business, but this time of year we are just putting down feeding for the lawns after the long winter nap. There's not much to do here, the four of us. Jenny, Bill, Jonathan and I take care of things during the slow time."

A voice shouted, asking who that was.

"Oh, that's my partner and brother. Nothing I can't handle, Bill."

A man exited a door she hadn't noticed before and she jumped. She looked from one to the other.

"I know we have that effect on people. We are identical twins. Guess we look alike, huh?" He said with a bright smile.

Grabbing her heart, she laughed. "Oh, my goodness, can anyone tell you apart?"

"Yes, said Wilbert. I'm the good looking one, see? Nice teeth, slim built, nice mustache. Fitted with dimples and a winning smile.

Martha laughed and agreed with him.

"You wound me so Bill. What about me? Deeper dimples, straighter teeth, bulging biceps, erect posture and pleasing personality. See this man here is a knucklehead, I am the brains of the establishment."

Wilbert snorted. "Easy, we don't want to traumatize the young lady."

She shook hands with Bill in greeting.

"Well, darn it, if I were ten years younger, I'd challenge your husband or boyfriend for you."

"Shut up, Bill. Even if you were 20 years younger, you would still be too old." Said Wilbert.

Martha laughed heartily. She was glad she visited them. She didn't get what she wanted, but they were friendly. Both men exuded joy. She looked at them salt and pepper hair, twinkling eyes both with thickening girth. Martha asked them about themselves, twin things they did, if they had ever been separated. And could they talk by telepathy. They sensed each other's pain and finished each other's thoughts. Both were widowed and not dating. They said they had two children, a boy and a girl, born days apart. They bowled, played touch football and both sang on the choir. Bill, whose name is really William, is an elder in Mitzvah Baptist Church. They live next door to each other. As children, they pulled the tricks on people even though their parents dressed them in different color shirts, would tell the principal who was wearing green and who was wearing yellow. They would pack the same color of the other twin's so when they got in trouble, they'd be wearing the same shirts and no one could tell them apart. The two men laughed uproariously. Martha laughed with them both lifted up and sad at the same time. She took her leave of them with a promise to visit again. She asked casually if all landscapers in the area are as nice and entertaining as they are. They said not really, they are the best. She mentioned she heard someone mention a husband and a wife team. They knew Esther and Jonathan Dumont, a nice couple with a small outfit. They are down by Fifth and Main St. She thanked them, feeling like she was living in a vacuum and was released. On this beautiful autumn day, she felt alive and meeting the twins lifted her spirits. They were happy and joyous. She proceeded to Grove St. When she got their men were loading a truck with bricks and fertilizer, or so it seemed. She did not want to intrude as they seemed very busy. Eventually the truck left and she asked for the owner. A short stocky man said he was. She looked at him, trying to imagine him holding her baby.

"Yes," he said. She apologized.

"Oh, I am Martha and I am wondering if you are hiring. As you see. It's a man's work here, lifting and stocking. Dotty, Gale and Millicent take care of the books, invoices and the like. I'm not sure we need anyone right now, but how about calling? In the next two weeks, people don't know they have to take care of their lawns to meet Old Man Winter, so when spring comes, the grass can spring," he said, laughing. She took the card, thanked him and left. She wanted so badly to ask about Esther and Jonathan. She debated whether to go back in the store to ask directions to 5th and Main. She got the directions. It was about fifteen to twenty blocks; she was told so she got a cab not wanting to appear tired and disheveled. When she got there, it was an attractive store. She looked at the waiting area. Nice chairs with coffee table and magazines, mostly on landscaping. It seemed newly renovated; the window treatments didn't look cheap. A man with athletic built came towards at her. He introduced himself as Jonathan. She told him she wondered at the name J and E, but now realized it was for Jonathan but who was E fo

"That's for my wife, Esther."

Martha laughed.

"That's easy, she said. I was admiring the place. The decor is quite nice."

Oh! Esther would be thrilled to hear you say that."

"Is she here?"

"Goodness no, we have a new baby so she is home, said a mother should stay home on a Saturday, he laughed. Can't blame her, our son is so adorable."

'That's so nice, I love babies. Do you have a picture? Martha asked excitedly. Her heart beat so loud she thought Jonathan would hear. She was going to get the first look of her son. Her palms began to sweat and a knot tightened her stomach. Beads of perspiration lined her forehead. Oh, God, she prayed. Let it be my Gabriel. Let it be. I will recognize him. Jonathan took three pictures from his wallet. And there he was. Her mother's instinct reached out to the baby the 1st. T Day he came home, when he was a month and his three-month picture. He looked like Ogwin. Thank heavens they didn't know him. She felt faint and swayed. Jonathan asked if she was okay because she was shaking. She improvised low blood sugar she skipped breakfast, but managed to exclaim,

"What a beautiful baby! my goodness, look at those long lashes and perfect lips. He is photogenic too. How old you say she is?"

"He is 3 months old. It's not a girl. But a bouncing baby boy," he said proudly.

"Wow, I don't blame your wife, I would not want to leave him either, she said. She felt faint. Beads of perspiration covered her forehead, and Jonathan led her to a chair. She felt her mammary glands jump start.

And the ice pack she used on her breast to stop lactation seemed ions away. The throb and pulse of her breasts told a different story. Hold on breasts, she prayed. Don't embarrass me by oozing. I am not able to answer any awkward questions. She battled her emotions; she wanted to scream. *I find him.* But she had to rein in her emotions. She grit her teeth very tight to keep them from chattering. It was a bittersweet moment. Her boy is alive and well.

"He is so precious," she croaked. Martha put a finger to her lips and touched his little face. Jonathan was looking at her strangely.

"Are you married? No. Do you have children?" he asked.

She hesitated, then said. "No. He looks like my baby brother when he was born or little. My mom would freak out if she saw this picture. Please forgive me for being so emotional. Do you mind if I take a picture?" She took the picture with her phone. She kissed the picture to cover the silence and shift Jonathan's mind because his brows furrowed and was looking as if he made a mistake.

She laughed. "Can you imagine my mother's face? I'll tell her remember I used to say you brought home the wrong kid. Not to worry, only when he annoys me. Oh, my goodness, I'll have some fun this evening."

Jonathan's face relaxed. "You seem to be enjoying yourself. I thought you fell in love with my son, but you want to harass your mother," he said, shaking his head in jest.

"Oh, Mr. Jonathan, do not take away my pleasure, but I fell in love with him too. Do you know my brother is Jonathan too. How you do you like that?"

Jonathan laughed.

"What's your son's name?"

"He is Peter James Dumont".

"That name sounds amazing. Important. I like it," she said.

"So, what can I do for you?"

"Oh, I came in to look at the decor. You have to admit it's very attractive. I wonder if you are hiring?"

"Sorry, we have enough staff right now", he said.

"Do you have a business card? she asked. So, I can call back to check? I am Martha Chime," she said.

"Good meeting you, Martha. Be well."

"And you too, Sir. Regards to the wife and Peter, she said pleasantly. So, I was transferring from Lehman College to Houston Community College. Do you know anything about it?"

"No first-hand knowledge. I live in Westchester, so I am not familiar with Connecticut. We commute every day."

"Oh, well it was just a thought. Thank you very much, you made my day," she gushed.

She exited the store with controlled haste. What a bonanza, what a find! A maelstrom of emotions gripped her and he began to walk. She was hysterical. She was crying and laughing. In between saying thank you God, thank you Lord, she missed the strange looks she got from people on the street. She was oblivious. She looked down on her blouse. There was no dampness but her breasts continued to throb.

Oh, for sure. That hymn was right. There Must Be a God Out There Somewhere. She could not even remember the complete line, but she found her son. Ogwin did not matter. He was her flesh and blood. People speak of miracles, and certainly this is one. So many things could have gone wrong today, the office could have been closed. But here she is. She has a picture, the parents' name, they live in Westchester, and she did not spend all day. She did not know which direction she was headed right now and did not care. Later, she'll ask directions to the station. This song adaptation from Psalm 150 popped in her head. O, Praise Ye The Lord, Praise God In His Sanctuary, O Praise Ye The Lord. Well, it was more the chorus that it reverberated in her head as she walked without direction. A cacophony of Christian hymns and spirituals clashed in our head, but in the end To God Be The Glory Great Things He Has Done won. Indeed, she thought He has been marvelous to her. Hours later, she asked directions to the station. The streets bustled with activity. Children shrieked as they hurried ahead of the parents. There were babies, infants in strollers, and she felt buoyant. She felt giddy. She knows now that she has done the ultimately the stupidest thing. She gave her baby up for adoption. Who cares if Ogwin doesn't want to be a father? She was terrified but, was it also pride? She just didn't want anyone to know she had fallen from grace. Will she ever find peace? Does she deserve peace? One day, through maturity, she hopes she can forgive herself. And she will tell Nana everything. She is the least judgmental person she knows. She would understand. Sometimes she believes she thinks too much. Her brain is always going. It never sits still, even when asleep. On these vivid images, maybe she should see a shrink.

Martha found a seat in the corner. She put her headphones on not to listen but to discourage conversation. In addition, she closed her eyes, but alert to her surroundings. What just happened? Her thoughts were churning. Peter, James, Dunstan; Peter she liked. Peter is a Bible name. It means rock or strength. She remembered her Sunday school teacher saying that. Mister Jonathan seemed nice. However, he never said the baby was adopted, but it fell in line with her child's birth and the fact that he looked like the father, Ogwin was proof. The child is hers but what does this new knowledge do for her? Does it benefit her or change anything? She really messed up. She did a great injustice to the children, to her parents and grandparents. Her newfound elation waned. She deprived herself of the joy of motherhood because she does love her children. Why did she panic and make a rash decision? Why didn't she tell Nana? As thoughts flooded her mind they found their way to her tear ducts. The tears ran unheeded down her cheeks. It formed droplets and splashed on her blouse. And as the spot widened, so did her love for Sarah and Gabriel. And so, it seemed, the chasm of her ever having them with her. She lost by her own hands.

As her earlier euphoria died, she went and curled up in her bed in a fetal position. She certainly hit rock bottom. She grimaced at how lonely she was feeling. Sasha came to her, and she told her they'd talk next day. She is exhausted. That she is exhausted, it's true. It is just that it's mental, not physical exhaustion, Martha realized. She must gather her thoughts. But what an extraordinary day. The following day, she told Sasha everything about finding the adoptive parents and seeing her son for the first time. She showed her the picture and pulled up a picture of Ogwin.

"My geez! said Sasha. You are right, he does look like Ogwin. What are you going to do about it?

"Nothing I can do. Oh, the records are doctored. I allegedly gave birth to a stillborn baby and there are other complications," she said.

"Complications. What kind of complications?"

"Have you ever heard the saying it's better you don't know something so you don't have to lie? This is such an occasion for your own protection and my godson and nephew, Gabriel."

"I thought we were friends. What's so terrible that you can't tell me? you are not an axe murderer, are you?"

"Funny, if I were, we would not be having this conversation. I am atoning for my sins by not telling you. I don't want repercussions. I love you too much to let that happen, to you. But you know, I promise you this that one day I will make a full confession and tell you every little dark, dirty secret but not now. I'm not an axe murderer, but I practiced deceit and I'm paying for it."

"Oh, Novlette! I'm just so sorry about everything. You know, you must make peace with your decision, or it will drive you crazy. Consider it as actions contingent upon the situation. It could be your thought process, being scared, unhappy, depressed or emotional trauma. In other words, my friend you made the best decision under the circumstances. So let us plan our next strategy to get out of here. Focus on our careers. Get our bachelor's degree in three years instead of four. Academics will get you through. Do eighteen credits, ace them then next semester take twenty. Agreed? High five!" Sasha said.

The friends hugged and as they separated, Martha said, "I must leave here. It is going to be too stressful to remain here. I love the place, but I must leave."

"Why? asked Sasha Is it more secrets. Come on! You are my support and best friend.

"In here we are. But the world is vicious."

"It's not going to matter. Do you know George Wallace and Jerry Seinfeld are great pals? I don't see society dictating to them. I don't believe a diva like you'd let a little tongue wagging that hasn't even happened yet scare you. Where is that Brooklyn resilience eh?"

"Okay we remain best friends because I do not want to lose my nephew. Girl I must be tripping. No way am I giving him up. But because I am an aunt, I have got to tell you this. My name is not Masters. It is Martha Chimes," she finished.

"Goodness! Do you know I had my suspicions? Many times, you failed to respond to Novelette. But why? No, you don't have to say. I know you have a good reason."

"I do, but it is simple. I did not want anyone to know who I was, and I was pregnant. So, I left home and needed my privacy. Away up here just hoping to fade away and chill. But I met a great bunch of guys. And thank you Sasha for loving me, being my friend and being nonjudgemental."

Chapter 8

The two friends always kept in touch and true to their promises, they finished their bachelor's degrees in three years. The online courses Sasha helped hasten the process. With ambivalent feelings about fighting for Gabriel / Peter, she consoled herself she has the address and struck up a friendship with Esther after watching her surreptitiously at the park. She played with Peter in the park and later became his babysitter with her husband, vouching for her how they had met; that she was seeking employment. Esther seemed nice and they talked. She wanted to hug her Gabriel their Peter close and never let him go. Finally, Esther relented so she became the babysitter. Esther trusts her and Peter so loving nestled under her neck. He seemed at peace and seemed so natural that Esther commented on it. She passed it off that kids seemed to like her because they know she'll spoil them. But she held Gabriel over her heart, so they beat together. She has to cement the bond. She hoped the hearts beating together would connect and he'd know she is his Mama. That day, Gabriel put his hand on her lips, and she kissed his palm then he kissed her and laughed was a picture she didn't see. But others did, especially his adopted mother.

She hugged him and told him how special he was, the emotions that gripped forced tears down her cheeks. Blindly, she handed him over. telling Esther you have an especially beautiful baby. She wondered how long she could keep seeing Gabriel. It was getting too hard to walk away from him. She loved him dearly. It was a battle she could not win. She was tempted to just take him and keep going. So, she quit babysitting him. From now on, she will watch from a distance, she told Jonathan one day that she was more in love with Peter than ever. That he was distracting her from her studies. Jonathan laughed.

With effort, she stopped going more than once per month to the park. She was glad when winter came, and Esther didn't take him out. She would go to the park and relive the time spent with him. She could let her heartache hang out, releasing it from its cloistered position. As the cold seeped in her bones, it felt right. Let it cool the turmoil within. She went to see Nana about eighteen months after she left Brooklyn. She decided to call from outside the house after watching it for half an hour. It was a joyful reunion. Nana, always in her corner, hugged and cried. Marty welcomed the tight hug. There was joy in the reunion. She'd missed the familiar scents of her grandmother, and her house. She always has baked goods, pastries, cakes. She loves to bake and is not bashful about asking chefs how they make a particular pastry or unusual desserts. Two years after leaving home, she visited her parents. She begged Nana to be there. Nana set up the meet without telling them she was coming. She was almost 19 and all decked out in slim fitting gray slacks with pastel shade blue blouse. Her hair was well manicured as well as her fingers. She didn't wear loud makeup, but Mary Kay's silver, starry night and smoky quartz eye colors. Carefully blended gave her an elegant look with delicately arched eyebrows and wore matte and shine lipstick in cinnamon. And all that glamour and elegance was to hide the clamor inside. It was crucial her nerves didn't get the better of her.

She and her mother looked at each other and finally her mother broke and held out her arms. They hugged and cried her mother kissing her over and over again. Her father was gruff, but she caught the tear in his eyes. He was trying hard not to cry. The reunion went better than expected. She brought them up to speed. She was attending Lehman College pursuing a dietitian degree. However, to be licensed she had to have a graduate degree, do a clinical. Internship and pass the national credential Exam, she was just shy of her bachelor's and will go straight to the masters. Much later, Jonathan- Calvin, Yvonne and Gabrielle came. There were screams and hugs and kisses. She brought them trinkets. She brought Calvin an iPod nano and shirt. The girls wanted iPads too, and she promised them on her next trip. She bought them gold heart earrings. They chatted for a long time. She stayed in the room with them. They were fascinated with her makeup.

"You sure look beautiful. And your makeup is really nice. Whose is it?" Yvonne asked.

"Oh, that's Mary Kay."

"I hear about them, said Yvonne.

"Really. What do you hear?"

"Yes. They give away free cars. I hear Miss Greta says her friend drives a red Grand Am and some other lady drives a pink Cadillac. Can you imagine? I'd like to ride in."

"You can but, you have to be eighteen before you even think about Mary Kay like that. Also, you have to earn the car. It is like when you get an A in school it's because your work is great. Teachers don't give away A's. Students earn it, likewise Mary Kay consultants they work for it," said Marty.

"I know that's right, said Gabrielle. I earn my grades. I'm just that good!"

Everyone laughed and Marty said, "I can see she is not conceited."

She spent the night with Gabriel and Evonne. They joined the sin of the world beds together and they slept. She cried that night. Those were tears of joy. She. Was overcome with emotions, she was unsure of what kind of reception she would get. Martin knew it was due in part to Nanas input. She spoke to her parents alone, apologizing for worrying them. For taking off, she explained she had a lot of problems and didn't feel she could share with anyone. She believes they are consoled that she never confided in Nana. Her mother pressed her, but she wouldn't budge. It was still something she could not tell them about. Said she's learning to deal with and accept her decisions without blaming anyone else for her choice or choices. There is a need to go forward and accept the things she cannot change. At the end of that, she pleaded with her mother to let it go. This sophisticated veneer began to crack and, in a rush, promised her mother to tell her everything one day; but not now. She would not return home. She will graduate in a couple of months. And has applied for the graduate program. Despite everything, her education has not suffered.

Martha's going home was bittersweet. It ranged her heart to leave her siblings. She could not endure the look of expectancy mingled with disappointment she saw in her parents' eyes. She now lived in an elderly couple's flat. There is a bedroom, a kitchen and a living room. Sasha visits when home from Syracuse. Melissa and Keisha are sophomores likewise Shaquana and Bethanne and at times they all crowded in that apartment. She has a pull-out couch and a futon. She always warned the Turnbulls when her friends are visiting. In addition, she would give an extra twenty dollars for water. She knows private renters. They are always concerned about their water rate, besides rent is reasonably priced. She has her privacy, and she gets to and from school easily. She remembered a conversation with Nana years ago, when she told her to be kind to the elderly and always offer help. She would always tell them when she went grocery shopping to see if they needed something. They declined, but she asked anyway. At times she brought them grapes, ripe banana, and whatever other seasonal fruit that's available.

Miss Turnbull made her carrot cake and meatloaf and soup. She laughed good naturedly when Mrs. Turnbull said she needs flesh on her bones. Young girls studying must eat robust. Martha helped to maintain the front and backyard. She brought Azalea's, rhododendrons and hydrangeas. She dislikes dirty places or dingy yards, so she took even nights to sweep and clean, especially in summer. She helped in raking the leaves in Autumn.

After the meeting with her parents and siblings, she started spending more time with Nana. Nana Remarked more than once, she looked different, but the same. Said there were shadows in her eyes, but there was a softness, something she couldn't adequately describe. She chided her for holding on to secrets better shared. Martha reminded her that's why it is a secret. It's what not shared as it would not be a secret anymore, she'd say with a smile while kissing Nana. Her grandmother sighed and smiled.

Grandmother, she said. I want to get through college, not just the BSc but graduates' degree but Ms. program. I cannot let the past intrude. It will be the guide but not the pilot. I am piloting the plane. Trust me grandma, the day the ink dries on that master's degree. I will tell you everything. Then you will decide whether it was something that should have been a secret. I can't venture there now Grandmother. I am doing my best. I love you, Nana. You are my favorite grand but I just can't."

Okay pumpkin here. Nana loves you too. I will tell you this, nothing you do will change my love for you, whatever it is. My love is without condition, that is the love of grown to know. That is the love God has for all his children. God loves you honey, don't shut him out of your life. You Can't Sing enough for him to stop loving you. Even if you think it can fill the Yankee Stadium, he still loves you. The same for me. He teaches me that.

She hugged her grandmother tight and said in a hoarse whisper.

"Thank you, Nana."

The reunion left her less stressed. She could freely call her siblings without fear her parents would be there. The biggest hurdle was her paternal grandmother Gertrude, Chimes. Her grandpa was such a nice man. She wondered how he ended up with a snobbish wife. She heard from her mother that Grandpa had a mild stroke. Through physical therapy had regained the use of his left hand. She decided to visit. Her dad offered to go with her because of the circumstances. She assured him she'd go by herself and hugged him to take the sting out of her refusal; however, she assured him if she changed her mind, she would let him know. Martha knew how tart grandmother Gertrude could be, but determined she'd keep her cool despite provocation. Grandpa Harold Calvin Chimes was a sweet person. He was not critical of his daughter-in-law as was his wife. At times, seemed impatient at his wife's snipe at her mom. His ah Gertrude told of his irritation, and it was for this reason she would visit her grandfather, nothing else. Martha visited on a Friday early afternoon. She wanted to minimize the possibility of an invitation to spend the night. The visit went well considering the conversation was stilted at first. Gradually the awkwardness passed and turned out to be amicable. She resisted dinner at first alluding she's going to her parents afterwards to eat, then relented. After more than two years' absence, it seemed right she stayed for dinner. She wasn't a vegan but didn't eat a lot of meat either. However, as she sat down to dinner, her cousin Charlotte arrived. She didn't believe it was a coincidence, but it was not her house. She greeted Charlotte, determined to be the mature one. Charlotte did not disappoint. She started with the same snipe when they were thirteen years old. Martha smiled. Charlotte looked her up and down.

"Well, at least you don't have a pouch."

"And how are you, Charlotte? You look well, she said sweetly. How are the parents?"

Charlotte blinked. She was struggling with Martha's air of sophistication. Her hair in ponytail, eyebrows arched, with Mary Kay eye colors in Peacock blue, Iris, storm, with black eyeliner and panorama mascara. She layered the eye colors using the blue at the bottom. Then put in the iris on top and blend and use storm in the crease. She knows the looks and compliments she gets when she fixes her eyes like that. Once the brows are arched, it is naturally a lighter shade. So, she was all 'sophistication.' She noticed the look of envy and anger flashed across her cousin's face. Martha could easily give her tips. But she held on to Mac fiercely. Charlotte looked okay, just not as polished. That's her, and mostly it was her application if she learned to blend and learn less is more and she would look really good. This smiled inwardly, thinking Charlotte didn't get a chance to go to Macy's to get an associate to do her face. She wondered how she could offer to do her face for her, without Charlotte taking it as criticism or as an insult. She abandoned the idea. It would not work.

"So how is school? What are you studying? Martha asked pleasantly. Charlotte hesitated. "I am doing law."

"That's wonderful, but I recall you wanted to work with the CDC. Changed your mind?

"Yes. It's my prerogative to do so, she flashed.

"Absolutely, honey. Simmer down. I didn't mean anything by it," she said, shaking her head. She smiled to herself. Those incredibly high heels must be burning her toes.

Grandpa Harry interjected. "I am happy to have two beautiful granddaughters visit when they could be on a date."

They chorused thanks and then went to eat. It was pleasant with Grandpa leading the conversation, quick to diffuse jabs. Martha knew, Charlotte's history but if she is looking for a fight she is primed to disappoint her. After dinner, Martha did the dishes. Charlotte declared she just had her nails done so didn't want them chipped. Martha found a pair of gloves and washed the dishes and tidied the kitchen. She was glad to be alone. She smiled. Charlotte still struggled with immaturity, and she wants to be a lawyer. Martha snorted. Good luck with that. The pampered heirs is in for a rude awakening. But you find out in time, she thought with a wide smile as she walked back to the living room. Her grandmother had tea, cake and cookies. Martha declined the sweets but accepted tea with lemon and no sugar. Her grandma asked if she was dieting and she told her no. She said that she prefers not to eat too much sweets and preferred moderation.

"And as you see, grandma what I'm blessed with in the back. Trouble is, it's from both sides of the family," she teased. Her grandmother smiled.

"Well, it's too late for me, but I'll just eat a thin slice of this lemon cake. It's my favorite."

"Oh, I thought, German chocolate was your favorite? Or is that cheesecake?" asked Martha.

Grandpa chuckled. "I can't keep. Up with your favorites. They change so often."

"Oh, hush Harry. Hush, who asked you anyway." She said with mock annoyance and smiling.

They all laughed. On that happy note, Martha made her exit kissing both grandparents. She said goodbye, she wished Charlotte well and hugged her. She could see the shock on her face. But they are relatives. Why the division? It just didn't make sense. She knew the rivalry was caused by her grandmother always comparing her dad, which Charlotte's and who marry well, which she decided a long time ago she would not feed into. She is a young person. Let the middle-aged folks indulge in it.

She assured her grandparents she'd get home in twenty minutes once she hit the D training. The iron express was quick, especially if there isn't a sick passenger. She often wonders why people get on the train knowing they are sick. She chided herself instantly for the unfair thought. That isn't necessarily true. No one asks to be sick. She'd do a sleepover with her siblings then go home about mid-morning. She has to study for a test and complete a research paper. She just couldn't stay. She promised them she'd pick them up their next long weekend and they can stay with her. Leaving that Saturday morning relief washed over her like a cleansing shower. She is learning to face the hard things. She must have lost a couple of pounds fretting about seeing her paternal grandmother. Knowing how she felt about her mother and the barbs usually directed at her, she was filled with trepidation. But she believed the civil reception was Grandpas doing. She did love him. He always slipped money, candy, a toy to her when he thought no one was looking. She really did miss him. She always listened to his albums, whether it was Louis Armstrong or Roger Whittaker, Jerry Butler, Platters, Aretha or Gladys Knight.

"All these young people just jump around and make noise. Can't hold a tune. Maybe only Whitney. And they Carey girl, Manacle, he said.

And as often as she corrects him. "Mariah's grandpa."

"Oh, yes that one. Marrah."

Martha smiled in fond remembrance, and she found her seat in the train. And took her MP3 player. She would enjoy some Whitney. Her small bag in her lap with her hands crossed over it had mostly textbook, crossword puzzle, and a change of lingerie in a cosmetic bag. She learned to travel light.

Martha picked up juice as she was low given the visitors from the previous week. She loved having her extended family there, she was happy. Each girl kept her promise to pursue higher education and each at college. She would graduate soon, likewise Sasha and start their graduate program. She would not stop; going straight and then find full time employment. The master's degree would make her more marketable plus the pay was more. She studied on the train, making jottings using trigger words that she found helpful in the past to aid remembrance. She was up late putting together the notes for her paper. Believing if they are organized then writing it would be that much easier. At 3:00 AM she went to bed. She slept until 8:00 AM. She turned on the TV and watched Live with Passion -a Catholic priest but, fell asleep halfway through. She is in the park and playing with Peter. He is running and she is chasing him. She is laughing. I'm coming to get you. He screamed and ran. They played for a long time. And she told him, "I am tired. Where do you get your energy from? She pulled him into her lap and kissed him. He said, Oh Mama, I love you. His chubby arms wrapped around her neck as she looked at him and she thought. Flesh of my flesh. Where had she heard that? No matter, she loved him, so she was glad she had her son with her. Just as she was hugging him, she saw a woman running towards her shouting.

As she listened, the lady was shouting. Thief! Thief! She turned. No one else was close to her. She recognized Esther and coming was Jonathan with a cop.

"She stole my baby; she told the police. Arrest her, arrest her. She stole my baby."

"No, I am just playing with him."

Jonathan came up recognizing her. He said everyone should calm down. He knew who she was and called her by name. He assured the police it was a misunderstanding. At the commotion Peter started to cry. Esther took him from Martha and she tried to hush him. But he cried, reaching for her. In the end, Jonathan took him, and he calmed down. He told her this is the babysitter they hired.

"You cannot upset yourself, so for no reason. No one is taking Peter from you.'

She walked away sobbing. Ironic. I am stealing my own baby. How can a mother do that? She cried and from a distance she heard banging. Slowly she opened her eyes. It was Mrs. Turnbull asking if she was okay.

"Oh, this is terrible. I must have been dreaming. Sorry to disturb you. What time is it?"

It's going on 9:40. We are on our way to church. You sure you're okay, darling? Can I get you anything before we leave?

"Thank you. No Missus Turnbull, but thanks for asking," she said.

Martha sank back in the bed. She is sure she wasn't thinking about Peter or Gabriel. She was watching Live with passion. And fell asleep. But it seems what you suppress when awake resurrects in sleep. She is sure her subconscious is working overtime. The dream was a recurring one and partly why she decided not to go back to the park so she would not run into Esther or Peter. For her health and survival, she must put it from her mind. It was difficult to put her children out of her mind. There were visible signs all around. The stretch marks indicate she had given birth. And she thought of the barely discernible marks, she thanks Palmers Coco butter and the Africans that sell Shea butter on Church Ave. by the subway. Those two did a great job. She can still wear a bikini without cosmetic coverage.

Lord, when will this end? When will I be able to move on? Lord helps me to move on. She cried inside, Give me some peace! And she remembered her Serenity Prayer and repeated it over and over until she was consumed with it. However, she made this vow to let Peter / Gabriel and Sarai know each other. She prayed the great twin connection she heard about would somehow let them know of each other even without her intervention. She remembered one Mother's Day when Pastor said, can a mother's love forget the child she bears or something like that. Now why did that pop in our head? Guess you're telling me it's normal, right? God. So please tell me what to do now. Then she started to cry. She decided then to find a shrink. She is not at peace. Then she wondered belatedly if the devil was mocking her. Can a mother forget the child she bears? Indeed, yes, she decided. He is mocking me, wants me to be tormented.

So, she said in soliloquy:

Dear Lord, who opened the blind eyes and made lame walk Help me to find peace. I pray that you will protect my children. That you give them long life and happiness. Lay not my sin to them. They are babies. Help me to let go of this turmoil of guilt and feeling of abandonment. I have strayed from you, but you are a kind and compassionate God. Give me peace and atonement. Send me a sign, you hear. Something! Anything! Just stop the torture, please. I cannot beat myself up anymore. You gave reprieve to the thief on the cross. My cross is children out of marriage and keeping it secret from my family. Forgive me for the deception- Wrong name, giving daughter up for adoption, hurting my mother and father, grandparents and siblings. Forgive me, I pray. Amen.

After she finished her confession. She showered and with forced concentration, wrote her paper. Much later she put the meatloaf in the oven. It wasn't beef but turkey. As the scent wafted into the kitchen, she decided to make rice with kidney beans. She didn't have coconut milk, so she used evaporated milk with two cloves of garlic, salt, Scotch bonnet pepper and Jasmine rice. She would remedy her no coconut milk status next time she visited the fruit and vegetable store. Grandma Ethlyn (Nana) always cooked like this. She is second generation migrant from Jamaica. Her mother's great grandmother Leonora Williams cooked rice with peas that way. She smiled for the first time, feeling light and content. She loved that food and the patties from the Jamaican restaurants. She cooked and ate normally. For the first time in a long time and felt normal. She promised to concentrate on college, finish and then start working on forming WASP. She will leave her children at the cross. She believed God heard her prayer and will look out for them she would for the next ten years. Let the children be she will love them but will not be consumed by them. The torture is over.

Chapter 9

Sasha and Martha finished their bachelor's degree in almost three years so by the time Martha was twenty she had her master's degree; she was on the fast track. She felt much older than her twenty years. However, she found employment at NYU Medical Center and was there for six months when she heard of a thirteen-year-old who was pregnant, and the grandmother wanted her to have an abortion.

Martha knew it was ripe for WASP to be born. So, Natasha – 'Sasha' Kewe, Keisha 'Key' Burn, Bethanne 'Beth' Lynne, and she met at Toni Roma's on Sixth Ave. Her one regret was she could not invite the Dynamos (Barbara, Sophia, Stephane, Jas or Max). She knew having a male is advantageous but, it will be decided later. They were all graduates from Forensic Scientist, Nurse, Computer Technician. Plans were formulated for how to stop the predators. They'd get information from hospitals and police. Martha and Bethanne worked in hospitals; Sasha with the police crime laboratory two great sources of information. They'd get a CB radio and police scanners. The tech guru would get that. They'd buy a black SVU and equip it with those paraphernalia. Next each has to go through rigorous fitness training- weights, jump rope, jogging and self-defense classes. All this to be completed in six- eight weeks, twelve weeks top.

"Ladies, she said jokingly, you need to lose some of those curves. We need muscles."

"Are you kidding me? Really, wailed Keisha. I love what mama gave me."

They all laugh, and Sasha asked:

"And what do I do with your godson Auntie Marty?"

"Well, we will rent a basement and set up headquarters. One person will stay contingent on the situation. Then we know who will stay. So now we have to see what other skills we need. Who knows how to pick a lock? Who knows how to remotely access a computer database and who's bilingual. We need agility- to run, jump and scale walls. Part of the training is wall climbing. Those reruns of the A-Team and MacGyver come in very handy for our operation. No use reinventing the wheel when on the mission, but it does not eliminate creativity, alertness, lightness and spontaneous action when necessary. Capiche? We have a gym at 14th and 5th Ave. It's above Jack's Children's Store. They open from 9:00 to midnight. Everything is there. I have signed us all Payment is in place for a month. The meeting place for a month. We take it from there. There are personal trainers there, emphasis on muscle tone. Say after winter need to get fit. Planning to run 5K in Brooklyn then maybe the New York Marathon in November. It's April and a little brisk, especially in the mornings. But we are New Yorkers. Nothing fails us."

"Here, here;" they chorused.

"What are we having for dinner?" asked Keisha.

During dinner they discussed costumes. Depending on the mission would be black or army fatigues. They would get an Apple computer, TV, radio and phones then operate from Keisha's apartment temporarily until they could find a permanent location. Keisha has an apartment W12 th St. right in the village, close to Union Square and 6th and 7th avenues. They figured the subways are an integral part of their operation. We will start training the following Monday. It was a beautiful evening of food and camaraderie. The prospect was daunting if they examined it closer, but their optimism was such it wouldn't phase them.

The group was determined to stop the predators. They are a group of women with passion; passion for justice, passion to right the wrongs. They are women on a mission. Those dirty old men that prey on young girls, as young as 11 years old must end. Their first stop would be W 4th. Park Courts at 6th Ave. Because of its high visibility. and basketball courts many children hang out there with hopes of learning the game as well as to get a glimpse of, if not actually meeting an NBA player. Greenwich Village, Soho, the whole area is beautiful, but there are rumors of abductions and a slew of questionable things. It is not unusual for illegal activities to color an otherwise beneficial are useful venue or place. Corruption stalks, places like that.

After four weeks of intense training, uniforms were bought, masks, gloves, computer and cell phones. None of the items were bought at one place, and each member made a purchase and bought in cash. Some things were even bought in New Jersey. Everything was incognito. They all wore glasses as camouflage. Martha heard somewhere that masks, same clothes give the impression everyone has the same height, thus confusing the observer, especially in a fast-paced situation. However, she doubted that, but time would tell. In addition, they are not planning to be caught. They would do the catching and call the police giving details and leave the perp for the police. They would pause and set up the scenes and nab the bad guys. Bethanne could easily pass for 12 years. She is barely 5 feet and slim. But she has a big bottom. Teased many times about it, she'd shrug stating it's her asset plus she cannot take it off to retrieve later.

It was prior to Memorial Day to 2008 when their operation started. That Friday night, they dressed in uniforms. Two in black and two in fatigues and miniature wallets on long strings slung across their chest.

Other tools were held in their numerous pockets. Keisha overheard two men talking about the score taking place on West 3rd St. in the village. Guaranteed to be a virgin and a blonde. They were going to party. She stifled the gasp, grateful for the potted plants as decor. She left and quickly told the others, so they rendezvoused by her and set out. Four determined women to save young girls. They stayed close together, but not to draw too much attention. In the end, they separated she and Sasha, Bethanne and Keisha. They'd use personal cell- phones on vibration to be safe. They would walk around but never far from W 3rd and 6th Ave. About an hour later, Keisha called about a suspicious black town car, tinted glass and driving real slow. They meet between 3rd and 4th and saw a man looking furtively around before steering two young girls, one with blonde hair, the other brown. Martha started looking for a cab. "Gotta find a cab, take pictures of the car and dude. We'll need to follow," said Martha.

Beginner's luck. They got a cab just as a couple disembark. Martha asked him to follow the town car, shutting down his protest by tearing a $100 bill and giving him half, keeping the other half. They followed the car to Soho Mandarin West Broadway. They knew very little about Soho. Mandarin. Looking at their uniforms, they'd stand out, but they could go to the club room under the guise of dinner and dancing, and then begin their search for whom? Mr. Smith is a generic name like John Doe or Jane Doe, but that's all. They have a weapon- Sasha. Sasha has a beautiful smile and uses it with the clerk when he says there is no Mr. Smith. She calls Keisha, who describes Smith claiming he hired them to perform entertaining a group of friends. Martha intervenes and shows him the torn $100 bill as a guarantee they'll show up. They implored the clerk, they are starving artists, and hoping perhaps some celebrity like De Niro may be there. The way she rolled eyes and clasped her hands, he told them room 252. Thanking him profusely, they took the elevator. It was on the 10th floor. They had not counted on that. It is clear more detailed planning was needed, so they decided if push comes to shove, they'll pull the fire alarm and run for the closest exit. They pushed a trolley knocked announcing room service and entered a spacious living room. Sounds are coming from the bedroom, and they enter and saw Mr. Smith and friends in various stages of undress with the two girls from earlier. She begins taking pictures and Sasha videos where Mr. Smith had his face with that baby. He would not want that known. Martha removed her. They grabbed the taser and the men got scared. They then led them towards the bed and tied them to the bedpost. The other two were similarly treated and tied up in the living room. The burner phone was left there for the cops. That phone was used to call the cops. They are unsure if they should leave the girls. Can they walk away from these babies. They decide to take them. One of the little girls didn't have underwear on, but that could not be helped. They used the elevator to the third floor, then down the stairs. They saw a sign that said kitchen, knowing there had to be an exit. They were right. Luckily the cab was still there. As they drove away, sirens were heard. They asked the girls their names and how they reached the hotel. They were crying and trembling. They were 13 and 12, Melinda and Joanne. They debated whether to take them home or to the hospital. When they tried to find out if the man had sex with them, they became hysterical. It was then Sasha noticed blood on Joanne's thighs and her eyes started to water. They had not counted on that plight. They didn't want to be identified. Their involvement was to get in, get out, disappear. How could they take them home knowing they were molested and if they took them to the hospital, they couldn't leave the babies by themselves. The uncle was a pimp selling his own niece.

Since the two girls are friends, they took them to Melinda's house on E 16th Street by Union Square Southwest. They use the burner phone to call her mom, Grace who said that she'd be home in ten minutes. They rocked the two little girls. Each WASP was quiet. They had looked at the situation for the right reason without looking at the effect on them. Their feelings towards the victim where empathy override common sense in that they 'over identify' with the girls. It was an extremely difficult night and task. It sobered the WASPS, and they knew they needed to emotionally mature. On the task, they must learn detachment to survive. They must practice restraint not to follow up. They must be clinical. There was no rejoicing. Furthermore, they cannot ever be identified to maintain anonymity.

After that night, they decided to plan their operations smarter, strategic, organized. They developed various scenarios of how to execute, following through and always escape. They agreed not to pull a victim once the perps were tied or handcuffed. They had found handcuffs in the Village in a theater store. Though not foolproof, it was tricky to open. They have to always wear disguise glasses, contacts and of course masks of some kind, plus hats or caps. Their second operation stemmed from what Bethany learned from the hospital, Downtown Presbyterian Hospital. There were two sisters who were abducted and assaulted. She heard this happened in Salita. Even though this was outside their scope of operation, they figured the perps to be regulars. If they are accustomed to getting away with their sick obsession for little girls, they would not stop; lay low but not stop. They may just change venue. Fortunately, they had gone back to revamp their plans of operation. They needed more uniforms, / costumes. They thought of Ninja Turtles but didn't want to appear ghoulish. However, they needed hotel housekeeping uniforms, automotive overalls, scrubs, waitresses, outfit and Burger King and McDonald's uniforms. They would also need press passes; something Keisha's expertise with computer programming will do. They have to get in the SOLITA and question staff and hope they are not too familiar with press passes. Both Martha and Sasha went to the Salita. Management was closed mouth about the incident feigning ignorance and that two detectives were already there. They are concerned about their image and reporters may draw unwanted attention. In the end, they spoke with a receptionist that was on break and two housekeepers, and the elevator operator. The elevator operator said he has to be discreet and when assured he should but, if a crime is committed, then discretion is out the door. Furthermore, what if the children were related to him? A twenty-dollar bill eased his indiscretion, so they have the name; Lister Giscombe, businessman of Woods and Bells stationery.

Mr. Giscombe has his business in the center of Midtown Manhattan, 43rd and 8th. Keisha would visit there to buy stapler, composition books, and whiteout. She'd be dressed as a schoolgirl with a backpack and oversized overalls to disguise her derriere, baseball cap turned backwards, popping gum. She attends Knoll Middle School, 440 W 53rd St. They hoped they'd covered all the bases this time. She should look for a security camera, security guards, number of exits as well as the office and, number of employees. She's to have a list of her purchases but set about picking the items up herself. Everything went well and she found everything except the office. She asked an associate, and he told where but she cannot go in. She asked for the boss and the clerk asked why she was not in school.

"If that is any of your business here is my backpack, books, white out staplers, dah! Keisha said rolling her eyes. Are you going to tell me?"

"We are not supposed to sell to unaccompanied children. Where is your mother?" he asked.

"What's your name? She peers at his shirt. Joshua, my mother is parked outside because there's nowhere to park. Does this store have a parking lot for customers? Then my mother can come in."

"No. So why were you asking about the office?"

"And I told you I wanted to talk with the boss. Well, can I use the bathroom?

"Bathrooms are for employees. There is one for the public and it's out of order. The last person to use the employee's toilet left it in a terrible state so we don't anymore."

"I guess that's the reason I asked for the boss. Let me ask him myself. Is it a secret?" Keisha said.

She is fast losing her temper. She would tell the others to let them get better equipment, to listen to police scanners like the ambulance chaser's aka lawyers. This is no fun. And the panty girdle she forced herself in, is cutting into her groin. She will remember Sasha for that. What the heck? She didn't buy her bottom, and it's the last time she'd wear it. School days are officially over. As she stewed, Joshua called Mr. Giscombe. She arranged her face, turned while chewing to greet Mr. Giscombe as she lied how helpful Joshua is and asked if she could use the bathroom.

The affable Mr. Giscombe told her yes and would show her were. He took the key from the hall and showed her the door. She went in and forced the lock to close from inside. Then she opened the door and shouted to Mr. Giscombe,

"If my friend Missy comes in looking for me tell her, give me two minutes. Thank you." She closed a door that was security he didn't break in on her. The beady eyes and furtive look remind her of a snake, but she needs relief from the elastic. She emerges and Mr. Giscombe is by her basket. She thanked him and he rests his hand on her shoulder and stoops and gets the basket with white out, stapler, typing paper and legal pad things she grabbed and intended to put back. But it is paramount to get out now. He asked name.

"Oh, why," she prevaricated thinking of a suitable name.

"I am a customer relations person. I love talking with my customers," he said.

"My name is Kendall Green with an E, she said, laughing.

He stretched out his hand.

"Pleased to meet you, Kendall Green with the E. Thank you and come again. Make sure you come again. Take a business card and you can register with us, and we can notify you of sales etc."

"Oh, no thank you. My mother is always fussing about all the junk mail she gets. But I go to school nearby, so I'll come by after school. Bye Mr. Giscombe and thank you," she said and dashed from the store.

Martha remembered Keisha's narrative almost verbatim. That's how he got busted by the police. It was obvious that he was smitten. They had shelved this as Keisha didn't get to find the office or find out if he had a private phone. She was hesitant to meet Mr. Giscombe again, stating he is creepy. They resorted to using their press passes to interview cops on the beat. Just innocent stuff at first, like problems they encounter on a daily basis. They asked specifically about runaways, laws that govern that and drug use and, suggestions that parents, someone could use to help these children. Sasha mentioned she heard on NBC about young girls meeting older men online posing as high school kids. They said it was around, but that was for the Sex Crime Unit. Asked about their neighborhoods if that was prevalent. One cop admitted he heard stories of adult males meeting girls as young as 10 years. The sick bastards he called them. He hoped they got caught. Preying on little girls was crossing the line. Martha and Sasha thanked him. They have zero information; nothing new, that they couldn't find out for themselves. As more and more households have two parents working to compete with the Joneses, more children are spending time alone. It seemed like PAL – Police Athletic League is broken maybe due in part to lack of funding as usual; and not many after school programs are available for these children.

With perps changing their M O and luring girls online to keep dates with them, they make composites of twelve years old boys enter online chatrooms. Keisha goes online and Little Boy Blue- Drax Calhoun befriends her. They talked for three weeks before he invited her out.

She agreed to meet him at Union Square Park, at 4th Ave by the dog playground. The meeting was set for Thursday at 3.30pm. where Little Boy Blue would meet Angel face to face. They printed the conversation with pictures and sent to both Pcts13- E21st St and Pct 7 E5th St. In addition, they called crime stoppers and gave them information, describing the 12-year-old- Little Boy Blue. Angel be identified by white carnation in her hair, white blouse, blue jeans ripped at the knees and a pair of air Jordan sneakers. Sasha and Martha would be there in blue jeans with a neighbor's dog. The cops are supposed to send a female officer to impersonate Angel, and they'd remain anonymous. Little Boy Blue turned out to be a 30-year-old man. He tried to deny it, but the meeting was taped, and he clearly called her Angel when she asked if he was Little Boy Blue. In addition, he had a copy of the same composite they'd made. They both took note of the arresting officers' name and Pct.

Chapter 10

They went back to Headquarters (HQ), very satisfied. They were giddy with surprise, totally elated. They pulled it off. That called for celebration, and they bought a Martinelli Sparkling Cider from A&P. That felt great, but they examined their work, and they would call and speak with the officers tomorrow and thank them. It would be good if they developed a working relationship with that precinct and those officers, even if it is secret. The WASPs decide to lay low for a while so they could visit and spend time with family, plus their annual needs for the Enchanting Eight (graduates of Sisters of Mercy). The WASPs discussed whether to involve the other four. There will be an open discussion of do you remember when we made the promise in placement. There'd be no pressure to join, neither would it be divulged they had helped three children. It's a decision from the heart and no coercion or persuasion can be applied or implied. The decision must be uncluttered. There are no strings to be associated with joining WASP.

At their gathering in July, it came up for discussion. Maritza and Isabelle cried off about last year in college. Some classes are offered only Fall and not Spring semester and the necessity to concentrate, plus they are doing Physical Ed in summer so they can concentrate on more important classes. Melissa agreed to join WASP and Shaquana said next year. So, they discussed physical fitness and told Melissa she has to enroll in gym or if she wants to do so independently, she can do that. She agreed to think it over, after agreeing not to discuss it with anyone outside of the Enchanting Eight. There's to be no flirting with the law; the goal is to rid the New York area of many childhoods sexual predators Martha reiterated often. It has to be clean, quick and in secret. They now adopt names. They would take some of the names of James Bond characters M, Q, D, RM- (pronounced Rim) and TD. Martha is M (Chief), Keisha Q (tech guru) D7 Sasha (forensic) RM Bethan (analyst) and Melissa TD (linguistics specialist).

The weekend passed and they met at HQ W 12th St. and updated Melissa on the activities so far. Martha decided to add some variety to their wardrobe. Melissa seemed amendable and was eager to start. They went to B&H and theatrical shops and got earphones, mini recorders and cameras and other listening devices and additional burner phones. It was agreed that two evenings per week were dedicated to WASP. In addition, duties would be rotated, likewise one weekend day. Weekends are mostly reserved for family time and household activities. Physical fitness is a continuous part of their routine. They seldom enter the gym together and pretend to strike up a conversation and overtime became friendly to any observer. Martha is glad each WASP takes their goals seriously and understands they can quit at any time but would be secret bound. There should be no disclosure for any reason.

A week before Labor Day, Bethanne reported she heard of a case where the paramour was sexually abusing these two sisters Bella and Elisa. They both ran away to Puerto Rico to their grandmother, and Bella sent a letter to her mother Milagros Collagreo detailing the abuse. Milagros was a crack addict and was unaware of this as she was always high or turning tricks to feed her habit. She had lost her job and now on public assistance. Bethanne said her source told her Milagros was showing the letter to someone in the ER at Montefiore Hospital. She had a bruise on her cheek and a split upper lip. She wouldn't file a report for domestic abuse stating it was not her boyfriend, Luis Manuelo who was the culprit. The social worker at Montefiore gave her a card and referral for counseling and as a precaution, made a report to the child abuse hotline once, she found there were three little girls in the home. She was unsure of what Agency for Children Services (ACS) could do. It was after the fact. The girls still live in Puerto Rico and basically, it's hearsay. Bethanne wanted to see the chart, so Keisha hacked the computer system and got the information. A plan was formulated to get in the apartment, persuade the mother to allow them to set up a camera. Melissa, the language specialist is ideal for the job. Sasha and Martha would be there and would pose as a nonprofit organization that offered counseling for domestic violence and sexual abuse victims as well as families. Keisha created a website, Family Benevolent Society – "When you share, we care". For this assignment Melissa was Shalyn, Sasha Gretchen and Martha Ursula. Once ACS was involved there would be referrals so if they got in early may be Ms. Callagreo might cooperate with them.

Plan in place they visited the home at 2571 Heath Ave, Bronx. The phone was not in service, but they took the chance. Ms. Callagreo opened the door. You could tell she was a beauty years. Now the beauty was almost faded as proclaimed the photo on the side table. Martha quickly made the introductions hoping they'd get out before Manuelo came home. She hesitated but when she saw the three beautiful innocent Melissa jumped into action. She addressed Ms. Callagreo in Spanish. She spoke urgently and desperately while Martha and Sasha engaged the children in conversation. Where they went to school, what was their favorite subject etc. They gave them coloring books, crayons, play dough and Goosebump books. There was a ten-year-old Carmen, eight-year-old Julia and six-year-old Alexandria. They noticed Carmen was very shy and kept her eyes down a lot but smiled when complimented on how beautiful she was with long lashes. Martha was relieved when Melissa said they got the go.

Quickly Martha and Sasha set up the camera in the girls' room. They swore Ms. Callagreo to secrecy and gave her a business card to call when in need of support. Hector and Jose have the other room now Bella and Elisa left. They moved through the building, exiting quickly but with nonchalance. They wore drab clothing, sensible shoes and Urkel's glasses. They walked a block; crisscross double back then got in their car. They were unsure the signal would carry to HQ but there was also a physical video for back up would up. They set up two cameras at an angle. Anyway, he turned Mr. Pedophile he would be on camera. This was the maiden voyage of the r emote video transmission. They prayed it worked.

What they saw on the monitor that Sunday night shocked them. Sasha and Gabriel were there and he was left to watch tv and play his Nintendo game. They were surprised at the clarity of the picture. He entered the girls' room and Carmen and Alexandria were on one bed. He removed Alexandria and put her on the bed with Julia.

Carmen began to whimper. "Please pappy! It hurt too much."

"Shh, he whispered. Don't wake your sisters. Do you want Julia to get some?"

"No," she croaked.

He then turned her over and removed her panties and inserted his middle finger. He held her legs apart as she tried to close her legs.

"Relax and stop fidgeting, he instructed. He proceeded to lick her legs and as she began to shake laughed. I know you like it. Look how you are shaking with delight nino. He then moved his mouth to her private and Carmen covered her eyes still whimpering. They had seen enough. They called 911 Gave the address and that a rape was taking place. Martha choked on the call she was crying that hard. When the 911 operator tried to get more information, she told her;

Mother***** send the police now. Is that your damn sick father you hesitate. I will kill that child abuser if you don't send help. Oh, my Lord send NYPD there pronto!

She was distraught. They were all aghast at what they saw. Martha walked out of the room and looked at the Manhattan skyline. She saw the tops of the high risers – The city that never sleeps! What secrets does it hold. How many rapes, murders amidst the bright lights of Jazz Clubs in Harlem to BB Blues? What of the Guggenheim, Rockefeller Center, Avery Fisher Hall and the Plaza Hotel with live bands and shows. What secrets are they hiding. New York the home she loves. But she could not deny the decay, but there is love and there is hope. She wondered if it was better she didn't know what happened to Carmen. One thing is certain, she will have to learn to deal with it. But dear father what of Carmen. Can she deal with it. That sick bastard. She hopes they reveal what he has done when he gets to jail and is made 'queen' for cell block. That-would be justice. She actually cursed at the 911 operator! She inhaled and she went back to see if they heard anything on the scanner if Carmen was rescued.

Chapter 11

They were a sombre group that discussed the ramifications of what they knew and saw. With the agreement of complete anonymity, they could do nothing overtly. Maybe they can pose as reporters again. But the equipment from Callagreo had to be retrieved. One or two of them had to go. If Callagreo tells the cops they will find it, if not they'd have to go pick it up and send to the cops at the 28th Pct. Luis is Alexandria's father, and she wondered how he would feel if another man did that to her. Would he be craving blood like she was right now. Would murder be on his mind as it was on hers? She asked a quick forgiveness for the continuous evil thoughts. The radios crackled and the reception was bad but it sounded like the cops were dispatched. When he was caught hoped the two sisters Bell and Elisa would return to testify. She prayed Carmen would get some good therapy.

Martha and Melissa decided to forgo Eastern Parkway Labor Day West Indian Day Parade for Heath Ave, Bronx dressed in sensible clothing. They overnight at HQ to get going without delay. They walked to Union Square and picked up the 4 train to Kingsbridge Station and walked to the address. It was pretty close. They have their bag to retrieve the camera paraphernalia. They met many people dressed or partially dressed heading for the parade. Martha marveled at the attendees and the areas of uncovered flesh that was hanging out. One young girl wore thongs and a wispy bra with a sheer nylon over the thongs. Well Martha thought whatever rocks your world. They entered the building and headed for CC1. Ms. Callagreo opened the door. She looked like she was crying. She looked more like a hag than before. She looked at her 40 years -married twice and has seven children. Crack cocaine was her master. It truly ruled every aspect of her life. It took her brain, caring, self-respect, love, empathy and pride. Where did that beautiful young woman go. Martha wondered if she didn't frighten herself when she looked in the mirror. The bathroom mirror appeared flawed with shades of gray. Martha shook her head to be present with Ms. Callagreo.

She asked how she was doing and where the children were. She said police came they got an anonymous call that a child was being raped. She was in the bathroom at the time but came and let the police in. The cops asked for her daughters, and she asked why but then saw Luis with his fly open and about to go down the fire escape, drew their guns and told him to stop. He came back and they asked again for my daughters. We found Carmen crying and trembling, her panties on the bed. There was blood between her legs. They called for an ambulance and took Carmen away. She came home a short while ago. Hector, who is 14 years, was staying with the other four kids but when she got home, she saw a notice on the table Children's Service removed the other four children. She began to cry. She did not know what was happening. They offered their sympathy but told her parents, especially mothers, should always question the children if anyone touched them, especially in their private parts. It's very important if males frequent the apartment or live there and not the biological father. Parents need to tell them about good touch bad touch. They expressed sympathy for Carmen and hoped she made a full recovery.

Ms. Callagreo promised to cooperate with the police and BCW (Children Service) as the nurses told her if she didn't her children would be in foster care until they became adults. She started crying again and the pair tried to console her. They asked if she told the police about the video/camera and she said no. They told her to call the police and offer the tape to them. It will show she was trying to protect the children. She was encouraged to take a shower, have some coffee and go to the precinct with the tape. In the meantime, they packed their tools and told her they'd accompanied her to the precinct but not go inside. She is to show the business card of Family Benevolent Society as they would want to know the source of the tape. They gave Ms. Callagreo a bagel with cream cheese they bought and forgot to eat, and she ate ravenously. In addition to everything else she suffered from Mother Hubbard malady. Her cupboards and refrigerator were bare. They accompanied her within yards of the precinct, gave her twenty dollars and watched her enter the building.

They prayed she didn't bolt to go buy crack because that twenty can give her four cracks 'fix.' Martha doesn't like violence despite her earlier anger but, she'd advocate violence on the originator of crack. It made pimps of young men and prostitutes of women. It destroyed much, so many. As a marketing strategy brilliant- bring cocaine to the masses cheap. Imagine getting a fix for two or five dollars. The average Joe (as they say) does not have to be rich to afford it and the most devastating part- how addictive it is. The mistake the man in the street made is believing Wall Street has nothing over him. Finally, they are equal. She knows the effect firsthand. There was a family that was destroyed because of crack cocaine. While both parents were high their two-half year old died of asphyxiation because the chest of drawers fell on him. Parents never heard the crash and by the time they missed him pulled the chest of drawers off him, it was too late. His death was ruled accidental but aunts, uncles, grandparents feud for a long time after he died. They all knew the parents were drug addicts. As the memory washed over her, a wave of guilt assailed her. What of the near abortion but for the grace of God didn't happen. Can she really cast the first stone. Martha shrugged to mentally quieten her thoughts. They headed.

During the ensuing months they kept their word seeking out the perverts in Brooklyn, Bronx and Manhattan. They rented a studio in Keisha's building on W12th St as it was so convenient. Almost all the trains are accessible from the F to the A to the 2 and many more. The Village is there too, Soho, Chelsea, Fifth and Sixth Avenues. Yes, the location is perfect, like the gym two blocks away. Keisha started dating and the crackling CB going off raised questions she didn't want to answer. What is she into that she's monitoring the police band. Was she a drug dealer. She left him go reluctantly, but that's when WASP knew they had to find a permanent home. It was easy to transfer and transport their paraphernalia at no cost. They could store more clothes in the closet, and where the equipment was. Inday bed the living room kitchen combination was there living space furnished with a futon daybed, tv, folding table with four chairs There was a recliner two armchairs and a love seat and coffee table. It had to have a home-like appearance. A single bed was in the bedroom, a chest of drawers and a portable mirror on the door. The bedroom door was always locked. Each WASP has a key but for appearance rang bell 6L. Their work continued fighting perps.

Martha remembered the "soft pornographic ring". Four WASP auditioned/ interviewed for this low budget film by Masters Manor Park. No one had heard of them but these so-called studios popped up for one to two years then disappeared. Masters Manor was in the garment district 1 W35th St between 6th and 7Ave. It was by chance Keisha and Martha were coming from Macy when they saw this young lady crying. She was dressed nicely and well made up. Martha asked if they could help and between sobs and cursing said she auditioned for the role of secretary for a movie with Masters Manor. The lead character started groping her and licked her neck.

"What sort of girl they think I am. I know they say great shape beautiful 'boodie' but, now I see why they say to wear a loose-fitting skirt. I slapped his face. Can you believe it? And worst I saw a 14-year-old there. I told her to go home, come with me but they told me to mind my own business. I am so mad. Got all dressed up for nothing. The nerve! Groping me."

"Well, you can file a police report. No one is allowed to touch you without your consent. Even if you are an aspiring actress there are certain boundaries that should not be crossed when it comes to touching. Where is this place?"

"1 West 35th. I am not going into porn I want to be taken seriously. I love Jean Simmonds, Audrey Hepburn or Sophia Loren. Yes, or the lady hat star in Ten Commandments."

"Ann Baxter," said Keisha. You have great role models. That is fantastic. On the road to your dreams, you will encounter bumps in the road. But I am proud of you. Do not sell yourself for quick meaningless demeaning roles. Get small decent roles. You never know, Spielberg may cast you one day. Don't lose your passion and don't give up. Here!" and Keisha hugged her.

"Thank you. By the way I am Jean."

As Jean walked away the two friends turned to each other and said in unison.

"Are you thinking what I am thinking?

Yes, we have an audition at Masters Manor."

They hurried home, refreshed and dressed in forty minutes. Both Keisha and Martha took a mental health day off and, to cement this therapy, they went shopping so it was an opportune time for them. They sent messages to the other three re: audition when and where. They took the F train to the 34th St. and walked to the address. They both had alternate driver's license (courtesy of Keisha) as Candy Dash and Amanda

Kerry. Creeps like these seldom verify age or proper identification. They posed as aspiring actresses and not yet unionized and dying to break into showbiz, the movies sooner rather than later. Their audition went well. They were given a call back for the next day at noon. Martha confessed she worked the switchboard at Family Benevolent Society and nonprofit organization. And she had promised to be there. They agreed she returned at 5:30 PM. The following day. It was obvious they loved Keisha she had big bottom per conversation with Jean. Martha decided to snoop. If there is a 14-year-old, she will find her. She sauntered to the back, peering into curtains stalls. She followed the sounds to a big room off the center. Several young ladies were hanging around in costumes, some had on leotards, bikinis, very short shorts and negligee. She introduced herself that maybe she would be working with them as early as tomorrow. Right away, she identified the 'vets' and the 'queens.' They had a turn up nose, heavy mascara eyes and that bored look.

Keisha returned shortly. No return reading for her, she is to start right away. They eyed the occupants trying to isolate the 14-year-old. Everyone looked so mature with big breasts. And then she caught sight of one girl that was talking very fast and too loudly. Martha walked towards her smiling stating honestly;

"You are so pretty. What is your name?"

She visibly brightened and said Renee Newsome.

Martha then introduced herself and Keisha. Keisha asked her which school she attended and when would she graduate. She said she attends Washington Irving High and is in 12th grade and would graduate at the end of the school year. Martha told her she attended KIPP Infinity and Keisha chimed in she did also. They just graduated and are looking to pursue acting.

"So, if you are graduating next year, you must be eighteenish."

Renee looked uncomfortable. Then reluctantly said no.

"So how old are you then?"

"I am 14 going on 15," she said with a touch of defiance.

Okay then. I'm 18, so is Amanda, so we are like your big sisters. Renee looked relieved.

"How did you come to hear about this studio and movie."

Renee said some guy came handing out flyers for extras in the movie; The Skillful Secretary so, she came and auditioned. The producer or the director said she would be ideal as a clerk typist. She had some headshots she used because she wants to be a model. She said her mother was helping her and she stopped. And she has an agent, Gordon Dray. But everything he got her was not right for her. She was an extra in a Coney Island commercial. She told her mother it was a photo shoot, and Gordon was there to make sure everything went okay. Gordon was aware from the beginning and encouraged her to accept the role.

Martha eyebrows lifted in surprised disbelief, but all, she said to Renee was I see. She exchanged looks with Keisha. A minor with no parental consent. Didn't even know what her daughter is doing at this alleged shoot. Some agents are dogs she knew mused, wondering also how much money he was getting from this cozy shoot. Martha had researched the precincts and had the numbers for them.

"Tell me Renee so won't your parents be upset if you are missing school?"

"I go to school and like today, my mom gave me a note to leave early, so I get a pass and left early today," she said.

"Okay then, said Martha. Are you coming tomorrow?" Renee nodded. "At 9:00 AM."

It didn't seem anything adverse had happened as yet and it wouldn't on her watch. She will place a call by 10:20 AM the next day, she will not be on location but will watch to make sure Renee got out. She is convinced that the so-called movie is porn. At such a tender age, creeps spread their corruption from the way the producers, assistants and designers touched and rubbed and patted you - knew it was cheap thrills. She subtly sidesteps the producer when he put his arms across her shoulders, reaching for a pen she didn't need. She figured that's why she has to come back and read again. Next day she will ask NYPD to do her reading for her. She would be risking a reprimand at work, but she had to do this. Her commitment to WASP is real. There are no negotiations. She hugged Renee, telling her to be careful getting home and to tell her parents where the shoot is. She said she would talk with Gary Stone, the manager, to see if she could leave. She watched Renee approach Gary and saw the familiar way he touched her. She started to pray for Renee that she would make it out safely.

The WASP met that evening. Everyone agreed that action is needed, and swiftly. Three calls will be made to Crime Stoppers 911 and Precinct 37, though more and more call boxes were destroyed, one will be placed from 6th Ave. and 14th, another routed through the computer and the last one from a burner phone. The first call will be at 10:20 am, then 10:25 am and the last one at 10:30 am. The information would be a porn ring using 14 years old girls. Martha wanted them to be caught in the act. She allowed an hour for assembly, dress and hair and makeup. She hoped it didn't backfire. Well, at the very least, Renee movie days will be over. And she is extricated from that debilitating episode while getting rid of Gordon whatever his name. It will be vindication for Jean as well. She hopes they all go to jail. Martha made the sign of the cross. And muttered a prayer for a successful mission. Martha places the call promptly at 10:20 am and the others followed suit at 10:25 and 10:30. At 10.30 a squad car turned up. She moved from her hiding place to buy coffee, bagel and cream cheese from a street vendor, meanwhile, keeping 1 W 35th St. under scrutiny. Her heart dropped when one cop returned in two minutes, but he went to get his radio. He seemed like he was calling for backup the way he was gesticulating. Moments later sirens split the air. The ear gushed out of her lungs, and that's the time she realized she was holding her breath. Curiosity held her bound and she stayed until she saw three men in handcuffs. Now where is Renee? Masters, you are finished, she thought. I will not cry for you. She has no time for vultures or exploiters. Satisfied she jogs to work. At work she texting WASP. They will rally Saturday evening, but maybe it will make the news. Later that evening, Martha could feel loneliness lurking on the periphery. Sasha has Gabriel, Keisha's son is living with her mom – (and now the apple of his grandmother's eyes). Charles Earl Burn spends some weekends with her; and Melissa has her daughter in a school near where her mother lives and who picks her up when she is with WASP Marty pushes away the thoughts crowding in her mind. She puts on her cycling pants and trots down the road. She will feel better if she does some exhausting physical activity. It will silence her thoughts. For the most part, she keeps her mind sterile. But Sasha and Gabriel intrude often. At times she looks at the baby girl and pictures her with Peter James. It's a vivid picture. These are her children, each not knowing the other exists. They are almost six years. At times like this, she wonders what Esther would say if she said to her. Do you know your son Peter is my biological son? I gave birth to him September 7th, 2004. Even now it haunts her. Unwittingly the biblical text from Isaiah 49 and verse 15 came to her. Can a mother forget her nursing child? Can she feel no love for the child she has borne. No, she can't, she sighed.

It was such a day she called her mother and was told that her old agent is looking for her. When she contacted him, he offered her a weekend shoot in the Poconos. It is a promo for the upcoming summer. The shoot goes well; the pay is great. It is opportune because the rents on HQ and equipment are pricey, so that income covers the expense. On the following weekend, Trevor called. Crest wanted her for an ad relaunching their Crest White Strips. She hesitated. Because they are monitoring some businessmen that have a thing for virgins. Her blood boils each time it crosses her mind. Discussing it with WASP, they encouraged her to take the assignment. She realizes if she is focused, she will not have to do many retakes and she will not spend more than a day away. Not. tooting her own horn. But the camera loves her. Her photos are always perfect even though not a raving beauty. She rationalized that WASP's costs are going up with burner phones, gloves, masks and high-end computer and tech equipment. Just recently they changed the HP computer for Apple high tech, high efficiency, high level processing capabilities. All the computer stuff is directed to and by Keisha. She often jokes if Keisha wants to be a hacker she has all the skills. Keisha said that can be her second career after Charles is at college or university.

With higher resolution equipment they get sharper images. They have better sounds for recording and voice equipment to filter background sounds, enhance speech, and a whole lot of sophisticated things she knew nothing about. They function and she is happy. There are current targets are the seedy CEO's, the well-dressed businessmen that give speeches and live in their penthouses with chauffeured limousines and plexiglass. For all their Fortune 500 status, they are pedophiles, deviants. But it is said it's a man's weakness that causes his downfall. There is a group of four businessmen that are very good friends. And if politics makes strange bedfellows, then pedophiles are ideal partners. There is an Arab, an Asian, an Indian and a Japanese. What a coalition of resident evil! They secretly unite to defrock young, 12-, 13-, and 14-year-old virgins. The younger the better the perverts liked them. On one level, she could see the evil and savagery of who they are. Hearts and soul cry out for cleansing. So immersing and aligning themselves to these innocent girls must seem in a twisted sense redemption to them. They have powerful political friends and it will be a desperate flight. Security is tight and access to the penthouse you must have a key, Sasha, Bethanne and Martha would get dressed up and wrangle an invitation to the party. It was crucial to set up surveillance in the living room and bedroom. Martha thought only Hercules could do this. And they are all crazy to even imagine, much less think they could succeed at such an undertaking.

These pedophiles are also notoriously paranoid, and purses would be searched. So, Bethanne tools were folded in her French roll hairstyle, the small bottle of perfume is actually pepper spray. The lipstick case has a hidden camera that would pick up the security elements in the room. Sasha's bracelet was equipped with a micro transmitter. It could pick up conversation from 50 feet away. But given the music and the chatter, well, they'd see how it worked.

People are always struck by their coloring. Sasha, Caucasian, Bethanne's swarthy complexion reminiscent of her Italian ancestry, and Martha's, bronze complexion. They definitely turned heads. Banking on men's shallowness they are sure they'll get in if it's just to gawk at the trio. The men never disappoint. Once they piled into the elevator with other guests they were in. They were checked but nothing was found. Their eyes travelled the living room and moved into the hallway and two other doorways. They went to the bathroom and then walked towards the door to the right. Hands on the door handles one of the security men stopped them.

"Oh! Don't be a spoil sport, I just want to peek at how the other half lives. Pretty please, Martha pretended to pout. Just a peek. What is the bed like? You can watch as we go in. I swear I'll only touch the bed, please.

As the others chimed in, he gave him. And they went in. They all gasped.

"Oh, said Bethanne. Call me crazy."

"Goodness! slap me. Look at the opulence; a heart-shaped bed! Is it one that rises and from a platform? Wow. She rushed towards the security. Am I dreaming? Am I? And you wanted to deprive me of seeing the gilded mirror. A heart-shaped bed pays to be rich. All of this time she's hoping Sasha and Bethanne are getting details and planting a bug. The security had to laugh. Anyway, it's time to go. You see everything.

"No. Can't I peek in the bathroom. Come on, please, I'll just stick my head in."

He was firm. "No, you can't."

"Alright! But thank you. I will not forget this night. I can brag I saw a heart-shaped bed that rises. She rattled on. You work hard so you play hard."

"Now out!" he said mock sternly.

Mr. Arian suddenly appeared. "What is going on?" he eyed suspiciously; Savarese?"

"Everything is under control. I've already told them. We don't do tours. And everything is off limits except bathroom and living room."

"Well sir, can't blame a girl for trying. How often does one get a view like this? How often does one see such opulence in one place? This place is gorgeous. When I grow up, I want a place like this. No prints on the wall, genuine paintings and expensive sculptures just like this one. Marble floors, isn't it? And you get to come home to this every day. Do you know I would happily be a maid in a place like this?"

Mr. Arian face relaxed." I can see how someone would be bowled over by being in a space like this. Sometimes we forget what we have and take it for granted. However, fresh eyes can put it into perspective. Ms.?"

Gretchen Cole, Sasha supplied.

And your friends Miss Cole.

"This is Ursula Payne and Dusty Granger."

"And how do you do? They chorused us politely. Mr. Erian seemed taken with Sasha and pulled her arm through his. And walked away.

"I never knew our sister was such a social butterfly." Martha remarked.

"Who would have thought it?" she said.

They laughed, but under her breath. Martha asked if they were able to plant the bug.

"Yes, and hoped at a very good vantage point," Bethanne said.

"Well can you tell from the layout how we can get in and out," Martha asked.

"No. I can only guess the kitchen would have an access. Guess we have to breach the kitchen then. Come on."

The duo moved towards the waiters. There are three of them. They struck up a conversation with the young lady that seemed to be in charge by complimenting the food and their professional demeanor, serving quality; appearing at the right time when food is running low. They praised their efficiency. They said they are Hall Catering at E68th St. She said they are online and discreetly hands them a card stating it cannot appear as if they are soliciting business.

Martha takes the card and gives her the okay sign. As she hurries to the kitchen Martha snaps her finger.

"Oh. I need some water," she said to no one in particular and heads in the direction of the retreating caterer. Bethanne obligingly followed.

"Oh. I am so sorry to bother you. Can I have a glass of bottled water, preferably Evian if you have it."

Bethanne jabs her.

"Ouch!" she said.

"Are you okay miss?"

"Yes, thank you Jean. Jean, is it?" said Martha.

"Yes."

She got the water, and Bethanne accepted a glass as well. Their eyes travelled around the big kitchen with a huge island.

"I am impressed. How on earth you manage to get so much food her in trays.

"Oh no Miss! Jean laughed. There's a dumb waiter behind the pocket door. We actually do some of the preparation here. The hors d'oeuvres are pre-made and finished here which is much easier to handle. The dumb waiter is accessed through the service entrance."

"Do you do many parties here?"

"Yes."

"I have visited here more than once and yet I have never seen you. With that food and the smell my nose would've picked it up," Martha improvised.

"Thank you. Well even for a small affair with his business associates, our host always wants us to arrive through the service entry. We will be back tomorrow for his biweekly business meeting."

"Are his associates handsome?" Bethanne asked.

"We don't know. We carry the food, leave it here and disappear.

"What?" Martha asked.

"We bring the food fully prepared in chaffing dishes and leave it. We do not see the guests," said Jean.

"Oh. I see. High level meetings-men's folks wheeling and dealing, eh? I gotcha!"

"I have another batch of food to go out." said Jean.

"Okay. Thank you so much. You are so kind." They smiled and left. They have a wealth of information and they have to go now. The business associates meet on Saturday. They have only hours to plan and execute.

Chapter 12

After they left the party went to HQ. Charles and Gabriel were fast asleep after exhausting themselves playing video games. The WASP discussed what to do. They know Halls Catering has access to the service entrance and dumb waiter. The waiters wore black and white but that was for catering assignments. They need regular uniforms to gain access to the apartment building. The doorman would know the routine and could not tip their hand. Melissa went to Hall to seek employment. Outside she saw a young man wearing blue overalls.

"Hello you work here. Are they hiring?" asked Melissa.

The young man smiled. I work here but I don't know if they are hiring."

"Is that your uniform?" she asked.

"Yes. Why?"

"Is it comfortable and do all employees wear that? she asked.

He laughed and answered" Only the men wear these and the ladies wear shirt and pants."

"Alright then. I like blue. Wish me luck" and she turned and walked through the entrance. Inside she asked if they are hiring and is told to return Monday as there is a part time position opening. She left with a menu.

They found cobalt blue shirts and visited a nursing supply store and bought bottoms. The logos and names were stitched to the shirt. They have security to breach. They would hang around and follow the caterers and once they enter would wait and follow as if they are part of the crew. They would have a trolley and carry some flowers. Somehow, they would have to find a hiding place until when the party is in full swing. Their equipment is a prop to gain access to gain access. Many doormen are notoriously nosy although it's part of their job heir entry is the service but, since their entry is the service entry maybe they will get away. Just to be sure dark glasses and turned up collar will have to be sufficient disguise. Unfortunately, Marty, Sasha and Bethanne didn't get to look around and get the layout. It is the penthouse and huge. They do not believe the kind of party with little girls would be in the living room but rather the bedroom. Well, that is why Martha always prayed before they leave HQ for their assignments, for safety and protection. Hall Caterers

On Saturday they trailed Hall Catering. When, two assigned workers went through the service entrance it didn't close properly so Martha and crew didn't have to pick the lock to get in. They hedged to the back of the building along the passage way and waited until they believed the lift reached its destination before trying to access it. What if the lift didn't open, what would they do. It seemed like an eternity before it came back. With fear they entered the lift with their trolley and put on white coats. Their cover story volunteers giving out free books and collecting at the same time. As they stepped off a door opened and closed. They did not see anyone but, the door is slightly ajar. The sneakers made no sound and Bethanne peeked and slowly opened it and inched her way in. Just as Sasha is about to enter the caterer's voices are audible. She steps back.

"Well, it's a small party and we are not decorating; just putting glasses, silver ware and side plates. We set up the four chaffing dishes, a platter of fruit and cheese."

With throbbing hearts, they wonder if Bethanne is safely hidden or caught. They wait and after several minutes of hushed talking and nervous laughter they breathe when they hear:

"We are done! No water, no crumbs, not a speck of dust anywhere! The cheese is sitting over the ice, likewise the fruit. By the time Mr. A gets here if the ice melts, then hopefully these towels will prevent the table from getting wet. Appearance is everything plus, he tips rather well."

First caterer remarked, "I could've sworn I closed this door. Did you hear anything?"

"Nope. Let's go. I have a hot steamy date tonight."

They came from the niche and rapped on the door tap, tap, tap, tap, their signal for any door. Bethanne let them in. The apartment is opulent but the business at hand blind them to its beauty. There are four bedrooms each with its own bathroom, and there around the corner another room. That they are sure is the den of iniquity as Nana would say. They have to get in. There is no handle, just a brass indention. They tapped it, pushed it, rubbed it nothing happened. They each began to search all over the door, poking and massaging until Sasha found it. With a low humming sound, it moved into the wall- a pocket door. The light from the hall spilled over so they could find a light switch. The chandelier looks like a bunch of grapes. Another switch and that is strobe lighting- red, blue and one with multicolor in circles and diamond cut. There are two love seats, three divans, cushions long oblong, round cushions, ottoman and sofas. The room is homogeneous. You could see small square tables, armchairs and recliners. The seats are red velvet and blue with gold. The room is eerie and suddenly Martha feels cold.

"Hurry Bethanne. Set the cameras up and let us get out of this room. It is creepy. I feel tainted and that cloying scent is turning my stomach. Can you imagine? They are bringing a woman's daughter here to violate her. Ah. I heard a country in the Eastern block castrated a number of men to curb population?"

"That's not really accurate either. I heard the same, but they sterilized both men and women- because they were poor and defenseless and soft. Millions sterilized and thousands died about 1976. It was horrible. But these need to be emasculated physically. Anything else is unfair. They better not call me for jury duty and it's a pedophile! Said Bethanne.

They set four cameras in the salon and one each in the bedrooms. A laser light will activate the salon; sensor motion will activate the bedrooms. Martha is getting morose and wants to get out. They exit the salon and is picking up when they hear a key in the lock. They slip in the kitchen glad they are in uniform. They will say they are arranging the platter. Martha grabs a towel and turns the platter with fruit as if examining for completeness, and nods as if satisfied. The chauffeur/ guard came in his face stern and asked what she is doing there.

"Come look! What do you think? Will it please him," she said affably.

He grudgingly looks at it and said it looks fine and she should hurry and leave before he gets there.

"Peace brother. Sure, I can hang around," she said teasingly.

Seeing her cheeky smile said, "Go on and get out of here."

They grabbed the cart and head through the kitchen door towards the lift. They round the corner but double back to look at the perverts. It is hard to pinpoint a pedophile. They look like your father and grandfather or uncle. There is no physical profile. Grown men; CEOs, Presidents of Fortune 500 companies. There is President of Tern Commercial Bank, Chairman of the Board Singhs Deushe International, President of Refentes Global, and CEO Drenden Enterprise. As they go back to the car, they park parallel to the building so they can monitor and hear.

"Guys, I feel nauseous. I feel sick thinking about to the little girls and what these men are planning. That is what you call lamb to the slaughter. They have no idea what these bastards plan."

WASP is tense and waiting. There is no joy, just comfort that tonight Mr. Aria and his friends will be stopped. Martha is extremely angry. They settle down to wait. Dusk came softly. The adults give the children games to play with as well as ply them with cheese and crackers. They are dressed in sheer nylon, red, and black teddy with matching briefs. They are asked to do the dance they practiced earlier. After the dance each man invites each of the girl to sit on his lap. A panicked 911 call is placed, that there are four babies being sexually abused by four men; CEO and Presidents of Fortune 500 companies.

Martha called Det. Roxy Haskins. She is the number one concerned citizen (Her code name to him used for years). She explained what was happening in the penthouse. Five minutes later sirens are heard, and they pull up. There are three squad cards and six cops. They were encouraged not to speak with the doorman. To catch them in the act should use the service entrance; go to the left- the side door is opened. Enter apartment through the kitchen; door is opened. They will find pictures and everything for the assaulters.

Martha is trembling. There's a little girl in red sprawled on the sofa being encouraged to do a split on her back. The bile bubbles over and Martha puts her head through the window. She stops watching. She is completely sick. As the cops lead the perps away about 30 minutes later, she is rearing to go and fight. Sasha and Bethanne restrain her.

"Get me out of here then; if I can't beat them or kick them in the genitalia."

They drive to HQ. Sasha tells Marty to take it easy and not get too emotional. She will get burn out. Great work is being done. They got four tonight and the tapes will help. Bethanne said the video tapes are just another step to convict them. She wore gloves so there are no prints. The criminals are caught. They should parade them on all networks and if they don't she will. The children continue to sleep and Martha kissed them both. Sasha said good night but, Keisha decided to go stay with Marty. So, they all slept at HQ. Marty sleep was fitful. She woke up in a sweat seeing her children. Both are playing tag as they run around the park, under the magnolia trees. As she watches a thing dressed in black with hooded face but with red eyes, blocks her view and snatches the children and fly away. She screams and try to give chase. Her body is drenched with sweat and her cheeks are wet when she wakes up. She was crying in her sleep.

A shower revives her and the WASP ate McMuffins and sausage cheese biscuit for breakfast.

"Who wants seconds," Melissa asks.

"Me, said Sasha. I love the grease."

"And me, said Keisha. I will repent later. Monday I will go back to tofu, bean sprouts, garlic sauce and pita bread. So don't give me that look."

"I didn't say a word. I just look at you as I always do," Martha said smiling.

After breakfast the children did their homework and everyone walked to Washington Square Park. On that Sunday morning Martha is quiet. First Presbyterian Church is on the same block as HQ and she walks right by it. The Dutch Reform Church is the next block, but she passes both on the way to the park. She quietly prays. She needs peace. Her soul cries out for it. Even though she is committed to WASP there is a void. Their past mission weighs heavily on her. Those nasty sick, corrupt deviants, degenerates where honorary degree is conferred, they make pretty speeches while molest, traumatize innocent young children. They should let them write a sign which states I molest little girls and have them on parade. It is almost five years since they started WASP and she needs a break.

Back at HQ they dissect the latest case. Martha is able to participate adequately despite her chaotic past intruding. All those years of counselling seems for nought if ii still so present. The other ladies are enthusiastic ready for the next assignment. They will rally if another case comes in. Still, its three days at the gym. She is glad for the physical exertion as sometimes it's the only reprieve she gets. Guilt is a shackle bigger than Mt. Everest. Its weight can certainly crush. And for the umpteenth type she said God forgive me for putting ego in front of two babies. You are merciful so I ask your forgiveness. Give me the peace I crave Lord.

She is lifted after that plea. She is renewed and energized. So, WASP continues its crusade. In Union Square Park or Washington Square Park they'd innocently compliment men of taking their daughter out. They monitor responses, reflexes, comfort, or discomfort. They would also indicate they have a daughter the same age. Thus, they got cases that way as well, or what Bethanne sees in the hospitals. For Martha she got from the social workers. She'd start a conversation you look beat. Information was given but no names. She'd later go with her chart and clip board and snoop in the computer. Sometimes WASP would be active four times for the month. Thankfully that was the exception.

For WASP fifth anniversary they would celebrate. They would invent another reason for the celebration if asked- Five years of maintaining the same weight through diet and exercise. Each WASP must wear her prom dress. Reservations are made at the Waldorf Astoria Hotel

301 Park Ave. They would dine in style. All the commercials they watched years before, seeing the well-dressed doorman opening cars for the elite; it will be their time. They will be picked up in a town car from HQ at 6:00pm for their 7: pm reservation. The ladies arrived at 6:30 and caused a stir. Each lady is immaculate from hair to shoes. They represent

the best mixture of culture and coloring, each a beauty in herself. They represent a bevy of beautiful ladies, and several heads turned, from the dark to the fair. And as they paused- it was a kodak moment, and a photographer materialized, and he took a shot.

The concierge offers his assistance and was told of dinner reservation for 7 but, because they were early would have an aperitif before dinner. The order for two Amaretto sour, Campari Colada, and two Cosmopolitan. Not schooled in what serves as aperitif or if it enhances the palette; the die is cast. They maintain a straight face when the drink arrives. They will nurse the one drink asking for additional ice. They are unsure of the level of alcohol in the drink. It would not do to become tipsy. They garnered attention for their looks; they do not want attention for what they do or behaved. Everyone is satisfied with her drink. As they toasted five years of steady interference of anti-defrocking of virgins, they acknowledged they did excellent work. Many times, they are unable to prevent the unpardonable. Staking out parks have thwart predators of their innocent victims.

Dinner was a hilarious affair. Melissa said she wants Duck Confit prepared the traditional French way; Bethanne wants well done pork chops smothered in butter, mushroom, onions, baked red potato and string beans. Sasha wants stuffed chicken breast with crab, wild rice, asparagus and carrots while Keisha wants sea bass with mango gastrique with garlic mashed potatoes and Martha orders garlic lobster with string beans and carrots, cauliflower with mango salsa. They laugh at themselves unsure what food paired with what but they are having fun.

"Garlic and lobster Martha. Really? Asked Melissa.

"What are you worried about. I'm not going to kiss you. You won't smell anything and duck? Really! How can you eat the AFLAC duck."

They were laughing so hard and having a good time they miss Serena and Venus Williams.

"Well, it could've been worst. I could've ordered frog legs and escargot," said Melissa.

"Phew! Are you kidding? That's gross! No need to give me indigestion before my one meal for the day. I ate rabbit food all week to eat guilt free tonight. Don't deprive me of my chicken and crab dinner," Sasha said.

"Yeah, and my well-earned pork chops. I'm so looking forward to my meal," Melissa said.

"So, whom do you prefer as cook? The ancient Julia Childs, Jacque Pepin or the domestic diva Martha Stewart," asked Martha.

"Well Jacque Pepin I like, Julia too. They work so well together. You know half the time I don't hear what the heck they say, said Melissa laughing. Hats off to your name's sake Martha."

"Hey Martha- think you were named after her?"

"Maybe your mom had great expectations to follow in her footsteps, said Keisha. Guess that's one shocked mama! You turned out no gourmet food, do you? Just ordinary stuff.

Amid laughter Martha replied, "You little ingrates! I cook a mean rice and peas curry chicken and oxtail. Nana taught me how. You can't get more gourmet than that."

They laughed at her outburst.

"It's just that I prefer nutrition and instructions rather than cooking gourmet delight or exotic food. My palette loves wholesome food I can see and pronounce. What the hell is confit?"

"But get this! One day I was watching Julia Childs and Jacque P. Can't even remember what they were making but Julia is talking about the roux and the roux-(pronounced roo) So I wanted to know what it was. I waited and waited, almost had an accident only to find its plain flour mixed in water and oil. Flour pastes for heaven's sake!" said Keisha.

The table laughed.

"It's because the French name lends an air to the dishes and to us Americans, it sounds glamorous," said Bethanne.

I love my name's sake. She makes a wonderful cobb salad. And that I learnt. I am so good I'd rival her. She really inspires me but, Isay people would confuse us – Youknow two brilliant Marthas in the kitchen. So, I just chill and give her the spotlight. No need to thank me ladies."

As the others laugh at Martha's outrageous statements the food arrives.

"Well, if the food tastes as good as it smells I am licking the platter clean," said Keisha.

"Oh Keisha! You'd eat it anyway and grumble," Sasha teased.

"Well, if you are hungry enough you will eat a hawk trust me, said Keisha laughing. You think I get this derriere from eating spinach? No offence Popeye."

While the others laughed, she sniffed her fish. "Thank you, Lord, for what we are to receive," and picked up her fork.

"Aren't you gonna wait for the rest of us greedy?" asked Melissa.

"Girl I just want to sample it," she said.

"No, said Martha. When you finish sampling, it will be a whole side. We know you."

"You are a real spoil sport. Do you know I hear this fish call my name long before we left HQ. (As the others raised their eyebrows) Yes, it called me then like it is calling me now. Never mind Mr. Bass. They ugly!"

The others laughed at her skill at telling stories.

Soon everyone is served. As Keisha picks up her fork Martha said, Down Keisha! We pray and hold hands; we are a circle!" And they blessed the food, giving thanks for health, strength and compassion for others. The meal was delicious. For dessert it's ice cream medley-eight mini scoops of different flavors with fruit.

When the bill came Keisha said, "Oh my goodness no. And I end up wearing a four-inch-high heels so I can't run."

"Mmm! Said Martha. I can see why."

"That's half my rent, Melissa wailed. I saw you Marty getting 'cushy' with the head waiter, I thought you'd be hooking the sisters up. I have a sudden urge to use the toilet."

Sasha and Martha exchange glance.

"Do you think they will allow us to work it off. I just had my nails done. These lovely rhinestones! Said Bethanne.

The look on their faces is priceless   and Sasha and Martha burst out laughing. It's okay. We got you. I told the head waiter to hike the bill. Oh goodness! This is definitely worth it."

"Okay Martha and Sasha, we owe you for adding ten years to our lives," said Melissa.

"Can you imagine if that amount was real! Keisha said, hand over her heart. Just for that you need to wash my hair and clean my apartment for two weeks. And one word out of your mouth, it's a month."

 Martha nods as she zips her lips with her fingers. Moments later she is smiling quite unrepentant. As they get up to leave the waiters appear and ease their chairs out.

"Wow! I like that," said Bethanne.

"Me too," said Melissa.

"Thank you, Henri, said Martha. Everything was wonderful. Point us to the ballroom."

"My pleasure Ms. Martha," he said.

"One minute isn't he Henry? That's what his badge says. What did you call him Onray? said Bethanne.

Martha laughed delightfully. "I said Henri. It's the French pronunciation for Henry."

They all started to laugh as they exit the dining room.

"Ladies room first so there's nothing in my teeth, said Sasha. As they walked leisurely to the bathroom the bevy of women caught the eyes of two French men, Peter and Andrew. As they enter the bathroom they notice the long mirror in the lounge area away from the toilets. It is fantastic. They look fantastic with only a mere touch of their lipstick. The dinner mints work but Martha has Clorets and Trident for each girl.

"You never know. A young Saudi Prince maybe there lonely, or a British nobleman just waiting for one of you lovelies," said Martha. One more twirl before the mirror and they head for the ballroom. A karaoke was in progress, and they spy empty seats to the far side of the room. Melissa, Sasha and Keisha who had beautiful voices participated. Keisha sang One Love (Bob Marley), Sasha My Way (F. Sinatra) and Melissa This Girl's On Fire (Alicia Keys). They got resounding applause. They enjoyed the singing that ended at ten, then a small band played a mixed bag of contemporary, rhythm and blues, soft rock, reggae, doowop fifties and sixties.

The two French men that eyed them earlier came over to them and introduced themselves: Pierre, Andre guests of the Waldorf.

Martha is amused. "Where is John? she asked Pierre.

(Qu'est-ce que?)

"English please!" she said sweetly.

He apologized stating it was habit to speak in his native language. "Why do you ask for Jean? he said..

The others are nonplused. What is Martha up to? Her evil twin seemed to have accompanied them tonight.

"You know, she said. There's Peter, Andrew, and John – the disciples."

Pierre is obviously baffled, but the others are catching on.

"I see you skip church

. These are Jesus' faithful disciples- Peter and Andrew.

"Oh, oh! Now I understand. It's only two disciples; they ran away, he said joining in the fun. There's general laughter and they pull two chairs to join the group. They are visiting on vacation. Pierre has visited before but it's Andrew's first time. They enjoy the night light of Manhattan. Someone took them to Club SOB. They like Soho and the Village. They visited the Empire State Building and China Town. They didn't visit their patron Lady Liberty, but passed by as the lines were horrendous. Next time that will be the first stop. They saw the Carole King Musical. They love the arts and Pierre studied ballet but abandoned it after he broke his left ankle now, he's a fitness instructor and Andrew is an artist. They became friends about ten years ago. Each girl identified her career. They are celebrating five years of maintaining the same weight.

"Oh, we notice you earlier as you go powder your nose, yes? And we were struck by your beauty. Five beautiful women! So, we wait and then no escort makes us very happy," said Pierre. He's definitely eyeing Martha and Andrew is looking longingly at Melissa.

"Would you care to dance," Pierre asked Martha.

"I don't think so, (and got a kick from Sasha and a look) ouch! Just give me" she said lamely. She glares at Sasha and bends as if adjusting her shoes. She smiles at Pierre, and they move to the dance floor. He walks over to the band leader and says something.

"I just request a favorite of mine. You will like it. It's a slow waltz," he said with mischievous eyes.

"I am sure it is," she said.

"It is called Je t'aime," he said softly.

Melissa and Andrew follow them to the dance floor. She and Andrew seem to hit it off much like she and Pierre. She let him lead. He is a superb dancer, and she has no trouble following him. The band eased in Want You Back for Good. At some point his cheek is resting on her head as they swayed effortlessly in harmony. Two bodies meet at a sweet spot moving as one. Wow, it feels good to dance again she thought. It has been years since she danced with a man and it is fabulous. She doesn't notice when the band stops playing, and the DJ takes its place.

She hears all the songs her father loved to listen to; the Four Tops, Manhattans, and Drifters and the gravelly voice of Barry White. They dance for hours, it seems until she tells him she needs to get back. He does but reluctantly. He whispered how much he's attracted to her and if he can see her the following day. She politely declines his invitation. As they ask the concierge to call a cab, he invites her to stay the night with him. She tells him she's not that kind of girl. She thanks him for the dance and being a superb partner. At his insistence she gave him HQ phone number. They leave the Waldorf minutes before midnight, hoping to make it home by then. There's lots of teasing and ribbing about Pierre.

"Sasha, I owe you big," Martha said ominously remembering the kick.

"That man couldn't keep his eyes off you. And you won't even date. You are a monk my friend Marty. Ogwin is the past and leave him there. You are beautiful, bright talented and loving. You spoil your godson rotten. It's you he cries after. You need to join the world again. You brush off every man who even looks at you twice. You just baby your godson-the only male you see. Can I have some back up here ladies, Sasha said.

"That's true," said Keisha.

"I date," she protested.

"When? Said Lissa. You mean the trip to the movies with George. Isn't that two years ago."

"Yes, said Bethanne. That's about right; two years ago.

"You exaggerate. It has not been that long. I don't see you traitors dating regularly except Keisha. So, you all be quiet," said Martha.

"Well, I saw him whispering to you. What did he say," asked Keisha.

"Nothing!"

"Come on Marty! That wasn't nothing. He was so earnest. The man was begging- Spill Marty, said Sasha.

"Ah right! What does any man want? She said blandly. Let that French man go sit down somewhere."

"Don't tell me you didn't feel something. The way you two danced- a paper dollar could not slide through," said Keisha.

"Look girls! Okay I grant you he is good looking, muscular and a superb dancer, but he lives in Paree and I live in New York Citee. He's nice to hold and I like the way he waltz. I would dance with him again sure. But that's it."

"Do you like him?" Melissa asked.

"Yes Lissa, I like him."

"Would you see him again?" she asked.

"Maybe- well," she said with a smile if he begged," she said with a smile.

"But the way he holds you close I just think you made a love connection. Honey any man holds me that close," said Bethanne rolling her eyes and shaking her head.

"Dancing close does not mean a thing. It's not a promise for a date or an extension for the night. Doesn't even mean a good night kiss. Yes, he said things. He wants or wanted a continuation, but I told him no I'm not that kind of girl," said Martha.

The girls started to laugh and laughed for a long time.

"So aren't you going to see Andre Ms. Nosy, asked Martha. Considering you all up in my binness?"

"The connection not too strong. He didn't touch my soul, because he seems to have too many hands," she ended with a laugh.

"So, you danced with an octopus, said Keisha laughing. Well ladies it was a great celebration, a little better for some," she said eyeing Martha. She refused to take the bait.

"There's another thanksgiving we should be doing thanking the Creator for our work with the children. Has anyone ever gone to the church at the end of the block. The Presbyterian Church at the corner of 12th and 5th is over a hundred years old."

"Now how you reach to church?" asked Melissa.

"Because it's a part of my roots. Anytime I talk to Nana she always asks, when is the last time you go to church. I just don't want to keep saying soon, when I am so close to it. When I am at HQ, I promise myself I'd go one Sunday. They have two services, nine and eleven. We can catch the eleven even if we wake at ten," said Martha.

"No promises," chorus three.

"Well roomie, what about it" she addressed Sasha.

"If I wake up and I'm not cross-eyed and can see I will go with you," said Sasha.

At that they separate, and Melissa and Martha enter HQ to sleep. It is almost 1:00 am. Teeth brushed and her face cleaned went to bed. Martha slept until 10.05am. She just doesn't feel like getting up but, there's that compulsion for her to go. She wakes Sasha and heads for the bathroom. Sasha is still under the sheet looking out.

"I'm too sleepy," she grumbled.

"Get up Sasha. You will feel better. I'll treat you to spinach and egg whites, two slices of bacon, whole wheat toast, and tea. How about it. You are not going to get a better offer."

Make it three slices of bacon and you got a deal," said Sasha.

"Done. Now go shower. Just wash the necessities. The water will wake you up."

They are welcomed by usher Peg and are escorted to their seat. They stare at the stained-glass windows. The organ prelude ends and the minister signals to start. The choir moves down the central aisle. The choir is magnificent, and the organist is no slouch, and there are two trumpeters. What a treat! She stands in awe and lets the music wash over her. Even if she does not hear or understand the sermon, the music is absolutely wonderful. At the end of the service the usher asked that they sign the visitor's card in the pew. They enjoyed church and walked to the corner grill and ordered breakfast.

The following day they got a call of a family in need. Their neighbor is babysitting four children. The grandmother is the caretaker but works as a housekeeper and is unable to pick the children up on time. She asked Joshua Mightiere to pick them up and watch them until she gets home about 6:00 pm. Ten-year-old Woodmere is to help the others with homework and watch them if Mr. Josh has to run to the store. However, he is sending Woodmere to buy energy drink, popcorn and gum. Meanwhile, he is molesting six-year-old Elias and twin girls Jai and Jane. The twins told their friends at school about the touch me game they play with Brother Josh and didn't want to play anymore. Elias reported Mr. Josh followed him to the bathroom and said he was teaching him to pee straight and how to shake afterwards. He also stretches his pee wee and said grandma didn't have time to do it. He saw him with his hands in Janes panty and told him girls have to wipe with tissue.

He told Grandma Burnett and she called the cops. The girls denied it. WASP posed as Social Workers from Family Benevolent Society. Grandma is ambivalent about the service preferring to change job. She will work from 9 – 2 so she will be home end of school. Six weeks after the cops left, she still did not find a different job, and accepted WASP's help. She asked Brother Josh to babysit the children. Everything went well for a week. One day he gave Elias and Woodmere permission to play outside. The desire for young girls was high and he was caught red handed. WASP planted cameras. The twins were crying and beg him to stop he was hurting them. They were not defrocked but there was trauma. Once caught Woodmere took a baseball bat to his shin. He was sixty years old- a grandfather. How sick can you be.

In July the cases came in rapidly. They had to select the more serious ones where ACS couldn't openly cross the line. WASP realized that homes/parents are neglecting to school their children on good touch bad touch. With the advent of summer camps and parents' need for placement for the summer that is open season for perverts. So, they contacted churches, camps, daycare and offered to give talks to these children. Many accepted and so they traveled the boroughs. Although they went in person, they were incognito. One minister asked why anonymous, and he was told:

"Children are innocent and must be protected at each cost. They must be allowed to grow and develop at their own pace. Molestation of one kind or another should never be an option or accepted. They did not ask to be here."

They left their FBS/ Family Benevolent Society card with number. They shook hands and departed. As they walked away someone said, 'beautiful women but, serious women, no-nonsense women.'

Sasha looked at Martha- "You hear that, Marty."

"Yeah! I hear. Certainly, hope none of them ever cross the line because I'll be merciless," was the flat warning.

They head back to Manhattan and HQ. There is a meeting scheduled for 5.30 pm. They would eat and strategize. There are three cases that need investigating. It requires careful maneuver as it involves a state big wig. This was picked up over the police scanner from policemen talking. Apparently, they were unaware their radio was on. It seemed they viewed the person as untouchable or protected. So, they were voicing their displeasure but, they were careless too.

Keisha had to do deep dive to unearth information on this man. They scourge newspapers, magazines and different media outlets to find out his haunts, where he did his dry cleaning, where he shopped, who he dated, hobbies, associates, social clubs etc. The difficulty is someone needs to shadow him, and they are all working people. The great Judge Earle Bradford Frondes has a penchant for underage girls. Well, WASP has a cure for such base appetite despite your calling and community status. NYC successful Sr. Judge Frondes you have a problem.

So, the esteemed Judge frequents Shades Total Gym in Chelsea four times per week and eats at Clover Fine on W23 rd St. Plan in place two WASP will register at Shades Total Gym and three would go to Clover Fine Restaurant. They would gradually strike up an acquaintanceship. They have to be divas because he was so impeccably dressed to sentence the drug dealers and mobsters. He is also very good looking- handsome really with a suggestion of wave in his raven black hair. Yet he is a pervert despite the smooth veneer of sophistication. Stripe the clothes and he is just a base adult delinquent.

The operation gets underway, and Sasha and Martha register at Shades and are haunted until they have his schedule. They wear leotards and tights or cyclist outfits. Both pretend not to notice him but are fully aware. Martha experienced a feeling of regret, such a handsome man with looks like a model; has a high conviction rate, a successful man in his own way, wrote a brilliant piece it is said on law and government nonetheless a pervert. Now she is hoping they are wrong. One day to get his attention Martha and Sasha start to argue. Sasha pulls a tape measure, puts it around Martha's hips claiming she gained three inches. Amid protest Martha said she did enough leg press, twenty minutes on stair climber and twenty minutes on the bike plus, twenty reps with the resistant band.

"Well, my friend you shouldn't have eaten two scoops of ice-cream. Now it is showing; What kind of friend would I be not to help you lose it?"

"You know Gretchen for one so young, you are a real mother hen. Do you know it is for the same reason I left home- to get away from my mother?" she said rolling her eyes at Sasha.

"Ursula, you will thank me later. Remember that red dress. Even an inch and it will not fit. So, start using the band. I'll do it with you but, just ten to your twenty," said Sasha

"Can you imagine, and you are my friend? Where's the trainer. He gotta help me out. He should know this because I ate slow churn, and it has less fat. She turned to Mr. Frondes, isn't that true?"

"It's a widely held concept it is less fattening. But I would not call you fat. You have a very far way to go before that happens," said the judge affably.

"See. I like him. Thank you so very much."

"Sir I'll be the one to sew her in her dress," said Sasha.

He laughed and held up his hands backing away.

"Why are we friends again?" asked Martha.

"You know you like when I fuss over you. That's why we are best friends," Sasha said.

They finished about twenty minutes later and set out. The judge is leaving and holds the door.

"Thank you," they said.

"Can I drop you somewhere? He asked.

"Thank you," said Martha.

"No. No thank you. She has to walk off what she ate on Sunday, plus this can be part cooling down."

"Your name should've been Chilly Willy," said Martha.

Saha laughed, "Chilly Willy's legs are too short, so that would be the wrong name."

They discuss that maybe they should not get acquainted. Martha tells Sasha she has a bad feeling about the case. But worst she finds him way too attractive and finds herself thinking about him. So, they avoid him. One day they followed him to a building in Soho; the apartment registered to Stepwell LLC. Other information says he lives in White Plains and commutes daily. So, what is he doing in Soho? It shows he goes there on Fridays because he doesn't work out. The third Friday they followed him. He was dropped off about 6.:30 and at 7:00 pm came out the building wearing tennis shoes and in full black; the shirt and pants hugged his frame.

Martha, Sasha and Melissa are in army fatigue, boots and cap. They followed but he criss cross as if he knew he was being followed. They stopped because they thought he knew. They sat on a fence to discuss the next move they saw him. They decided to follow. This time they walked slower and mingled with other – faces indistinct. Martha told the others to take W Houston St- turn on Wooster to Spring St and she'd give them time to walk there, and she will walk back down Spring Street and go to Wooster.

When Martha waited long enough and did not see Sasha and Melissa, she rounded the corner and see a teenage girl plunge a knife in Judge Frontes.

"No! she cried. Do not kill him. She grabbed the girl's hand and push and blocks the next swing and the knife cuts her. Please spare him."

"This s o b has been having sex with me for three months now. My uncle said to be nice to him. But I beg him to stop.

Okay, okay what's your name. You only stab him."

Dral. I hit him with a rock and, and"

"Okay go. Run. Go"

She bends over Judge Frondes. He is bleeding from the blow in the head and stomach and his stomach. She is paralyzed and can't move.

"Oh Judge, oh Judge she said silently.

His glazed eyes looked at her. She held his head and called 911.

"Help! Somebody. Get the ambulance. Help! Call the police."

The others hear her and come running up the alley, wanting to know what happened. She briefly tells them then instructs them to go. Go the way they came. She will call for help again but, WASP can't be compromised. She will shout for help then they can come back with the crowd. She shouts for help. She calls 911 again. A beat cop hears and comes and asked her what happened, she explains as best she can. Sirens are screaming now. As two squad cars come, and she recounts the events again she intercepts a look between the cops. The ambulance carries him to Downtown Hospital. She is covered in his blood. It is a while before she notices the burning on the outer side of her right hand.

"Oh shucks! She cut me when I tried to stop her killing the Judge," Martha said.

Officer Pool eyes lit up. "Do you know him?"

"I know who he is," she said. She must be very careful because she hates lies. She knows how lies beget lies.

"What does that mean?" Officer Poole asked.

"It's like knowing who Patrick Ewing s nor acquaintances or Micheal Jordan is. We are not friends. I see him on the news in magazines like that.

Officer Poole turns to her. "You should get that hand looked after. And we will need to talk with you some more."

Martha walks away going towards where Melissa is standing. Her eyes search for Sasha and she is talking with a slim boy. She turned and coming towards Martha and exclaimed:

"Marty you are covered with blood. Your hand is bleeding. You need to go to the hospital and get a tetanus shot."

"Yes, I will go to the hospital just in case."

Melissa takes her bandana from her pocket and makes a tourniquet and they set off to Downtown Hospital. With the congestion of squad cars, the trio head for Lafayette St. to take them to William St. Maybe away from the crowd they would find a cab. They dare not go back to the car for fear someone may recognize them. While they wait in the ER Melissa will go get the car drive to the hospital Sasha will announce someone bleeding badly and see if they will be seen immediately. That should buy leverage. That done she is carried inside. She asked about the injured man that just arrived stating she found him, prevented a second stab and called 911. She only realized she was bleeding.

Chapter 13

udge Earle Bradford Frondes died. He died on the operating table. He bled out. There was extensive internal bleeding. Martha gave her correct address to shield the others from getting involved with the investigation. The explanation- a visit to Soho/Tribeca and stroll around. They would go to eat afterwards at Lanbridge. However, they would take separate route, and the last person would pay for all the meals. They separated at Dalia's Idyllic sells costume jewelry hence they were not together. They came running when they heard her shout.

Martha was not sure why the retrospection. Martha thought back to her years in prison. She stayed in shock for two years. She was ganged at Bedford Hill and had not fought back which earned her special privilege. The Warden was a tall middle-aged gentleman with kind-tired eyes. He interviewed her and she told him what happened, but asked that none be punished for it, so they had an understanding. She told him she never killed Frondes, had no reason. He recommended an appeals lawyer, but she did not believe he would expend the time and effort fearing he wouldn't be paid for his service. During the long, lonely nights she reflected on her life and her mistakes. She wished she could start over again. She began praying to the God of her early youth, the God she believed in who gave her the bike, the doll; the God that said suffer little children to come unto me, the God before Ogwin. She listened to Father Cederic Pisegna and Joel Osteen. She wrote to Father Cederic and Joel for free books. She got You are Loved, Your best Life Now and many more.

Martha started back on the life she once knew, before she was side tracked by ego and men. One day Joel talked about a friend who had killed and waiting for a gift got a Bible. He was angry, he had no use for it but he couldn't get rid of it so he read it, got converted and became a Christian and was miraculously released and now a minister. She realized God never left. She turned her back on Him. She found the salvation she needed. They have a group that meet and worship Sundays and Wednesday. Her faith is renewed and awaits liberation from the four walls. But her mind is free and she still gets concession from the warder.

There is a salon where they can give each other shampoos, perms and styling. There's a blow dryer, and curler and flat comb used under supervision. She got them to amend the diet without spending additional funds. She volunteered in the kitchen making tasty treats for everyone- making egg-less cakes, plus cookies, making cake with only apples and raisons for sugar so the diabetics can have some sweets without sweets. She got the Warden to allow regular clothes for inside and outside instructors. Inmates are allowed to have their hair done before a visit, especially from their children and allow visits in a recreational room for children under ten. Martha encouraged the women to free their mind and don't remain trapped. She encouraged them to attend the GED classes. She taught English, Mathematics and Global studies. Many were successful. She felt good going to the parole Board/Hearing. Her behavior is outstanding. She has positive effects on the other inmates with her leadership skills and different initiates undertaken by her and reduction of gangs and cliques. She even started a choir and have half hour concerts.

Her WASP identity was not far from her and intact. She along with two other inmates got three guards tossed for preying on the women for sexual favors. Unbeknown to him the Warden was listening. However, she was hoping this would not come up at the hearing and she would make it through. She was warned about hard heart Hangle. She was tough as nails. One little slip and you were back in your cell for years. She ruled every panel she is on.

Martha prayed again that she is paroled. Her faith is solid and as the door opens, she notices the panel of five. And she told herself courage girl; God's got you and she walked confidently towards them. God, please soften Hangle's heart. The broad face Hangle is wearing a grey suit with breasts jutting out. The bottle blonde has her hair piled high on her head held together with hair spray and red lipstick. Martha did not twitch. Her face is bland and does not reveal what she is thinking. The interview started after the introductions. Each panelist has a file on her. She is quiet. Mr. Green spoke first commenting on her work and motivation. She answered honestly and with conviction. Mr. Suterene and Phaltank pushed on what she learnt in confinement.

Then the dreaded Hangle started, why should she be released and what benefit can she be to society. Martha inhales and slowly answers. Her voice is clear, respectful and resolute. She doesn't flinch or waver from Hangle's stare as she asks about her associates in the judge's murder. She calmly responds she does not understand the question. She is referring to person, or persons involved with the murder. Her response there are no associates that she knows of; that the death of Judge Frondes was rash, thoughtless, unkind and horrible. She accepts responsibility and hopes she will be forgiven. Given the opportunity will redirect others, work passionately to stem violence and stress the importance and value of a person's life. After more questions about her personal plans/

employment and volunteer opportunities. She will go back to school. She was promised a response in ten days.

The following day she asked the Warden to call Det Woods at 28th Pct a request to visit her. He said he cannot visit but will call at 3:00 pm. Martha reminded him of his promises to search for the knife and the DNA under the Judge's fingernail. She thanks him and walks back to her room. At least she has prayer meeting this evening. She chose this: We have come into His house, gathered in his name to worship him (Repeat)

We have come into His house, Gathered in His name to worship Christ the Lord Worship Him Jesus Christ the Lord.

She concentrates on the worship but prayed for forgiveness in admitting to a crime she didn't commit. She'd always hoped the girl could come forward but, she cannot blame her. Poor kid, adult now. She is getting out. She called her mother to rent a room somewhere for her. Next day she told her mother she changed her mind. She will call Nana and ask her if she can stay with her. She calls Nana and asks her although there's another three days to go, she is confident she will be paroled. Her mind is already free. She was summoned to the Warden.

"Well, my dear, it is official. Your parole is granted. You will leave on Friday. It will give you enough time to say goodbyes. Thank you for your leadership. I hope you can clear your name. You are still young and beautiful; you will find a job. And until otherwise stated comply with the Parole Officer (P O). Don't be provoked. Your time here, your behavior, just excellent! Walk in your destiny my child. God bless and good luck," he said shaking her hand.

"Thank you, Warden. I appreciate all you did for me. Thank you for not judging me. I will not let you down. I will clear my name, and I will make you proud." She hugs him.

Thank you, Lord, for remembering me. Thank you, Lord I get to go home. Thank you, Lord I will reconnect to parents, siblings, family friends. Five years ago, she made a hard decision to stop her parents and everyone. It was too hard on her parents and her godson and nephews. Her parents call and send letters. Denise sends letters and anecdotes and birthday cards from Johnathan. Her decision to stay by Nana is to avoid awkwardness for parents, siblings and grandparents. It must've been a nightmare for them at school.

On Friday she said goodbyes. There are tears and real affection and emotions. She encouraged them to stay clean and positive, study hard and pass their GED. Soon they will be learning skills. She will come back to visit and teach when she can. She left and walked right in the arms of Nana. Nana continued to visit every six months even when she told her not to. It took forty minutes to reach home. Nana has jerk chicken, oxtail, rice and peas, carrot and cucumber juice. She goes to the bathroom and strips, while filling the tub. She needs a good soak.

After the meal she talks to Nana for hours. She told her everything about her pregnancy, aborted abortion, and putting the baby girl up for adoption. She also reveals the theft of her baby boy. She had no prenatal care until the sixth month and the doctor who saw her never told her. She would never consider adoption if she knew she was carrying twins. The little girl she asked the adopted parents to name her Sarai and gave them a bracelet. Without this agreement then she'd reneged. At first the doctor denied a second child, then said he was still born but I heard him cry. So, I got the name of the ladies' that gave birth and track my son. He stole Ethan Gabriel and sold him to a lady with the stillborn son. They gave me the stillborn son. But I know him and his parents and used to have pictures of him on my phone. His parents are Esther and Johnathan Dunston and live in Westchester.

"There's more Grandma. I had the children under an assumed name, Novelette Masters."

"You did what? Asks Nana and makes the sign of the cross. Holy Mary pray for us sinners. Martha Chimes I feel like paddling your backside. Why you do a fool thing like that. How many times did I ask you? You know I would do anything for you. You used to rust me but once you took up with that Hispanic boy, you changed. So, I have two great-grand children I will never meet. Oh, pumpkin why didn't you come to me."

Nana's face crumbled and tears glistened, then rolled down her cheeks. Then she turns and hugs Martha. "I am sorry Marty. I am sorry for your loss. Now I understand the shadows and deep pool I noticed ten years ago. Chile you should've shared rather than carry that burden."

Martha feels better. She is glad she is coming clean. She cannot serve two masters. Confession is the only recourse opened to her. She tells Nana she will take her to the park one day and maybe will see Gabriel/ Peter. Unsure how his parents will react due to her conviction. She has not seen Peter in twelve years and now a teenager and she doesn't know if she can tell the parents he's her child stolen from her. Nana tells her to pray about it and leave the request with Jesus.

She called the WASP line and left a message. Alpha the eagle has landed. And in code asked to meet in Westchester Park at 2 at the NE corner by the gazebo. Martha takes Nana to the park at 1:00pm. Esther is not there. There are a group of boys playing soccer. She walks around none looks like Ogwin. She hears Hey wait up. Her heart skips a beat Ogwin! But it's not but a younger version of him. His features change a little but he still looks like Ogwin.

"Halo Peter. How are you? Wow. Look how you have grown!"

"Yes, hi. I don't remember you, he said.

"I knew you when you were about two/three years old. You have not changed much. Tell Esther and Johathan, Martha says hello. I'm the one that fell in love with their son and has a brother named Johnathan, said Martha. Oh, this is my Nana – grandmother."

"Hi Nana," he said head down.

"Just saying hello. Go join your friends.

"Bye Martha, bye mam," he said trotting off.

All WASP turn up. They hug, kiss, laugh and cry. Nana is introduced.

"Gabriel will be mad he is missing you. I did not tell him," Said Sasha.

"And I didn't tell Charles either," said Keisha.

"I would love to see my nephews," said Martha. Then she turns to Nana, these are the friends I told you about. We have been friends since we were sixteen.

"Nice to meet you ladies. Marty, I know you have to catch up with your friends, so when you are finished you can all come by. I have fresh pork chops and chicken."

"Thank you, Nana, we will," they said.

They lower their voices to discuss WASP. Operations scale way back. They kept HQ but are they continuing.

"Marty you were the heart of this and when you left, we took on less and less. We still call the precinct, set up the cameras. We do one case every six months. We still work incognito and respond to requests. Are you ready to resume," said Melissa.

"I love you guys but can't jump back in immediately. Let me get a rest, then regroup," said Martha.

"Well didn't you get enough rest at Bedford Hills country club, asked Keisha. Hear tell you were in the lap of luxury."

Everyone laughs.

Thank you, Key. I have to think of my role in wasp. I have my to clear my name. I have already called Det. Woods. I told him about the scratches on the girl's cheek and to check the judge's fingernails. He promised to review his notes. The quack I had for a lawyer didn't bring it up. I'd been wounded on my right hand and each time I brought it up he nodded or shushed me. I am going to call my cousin Charlotte to handle things for me. Plus, I'm restricted with travel. I have curfew. Get me a burner phone. I'll work remotely in a limited way. But know the irony about this? I liked him, felt drawn to him. Wished I could've said don't go that way. Guessed I lacked the courage, go figure!"

"Geez Marty, I am sorry," said Sasha.

"No matter. It's water under the bridge. Such a handsome man! I met his mother and sister. Told them I did not kill him- have no reason to because I did not know him. I would lack the courage to do that. He was much too handsome to go like that. I think they believe me, she said softly.

A quiet hung over the gazebo. Each WASP seemed lost in thoughts until Keisha said she was hungry.

"Me too. I can smell those pork chops," said Bethanne.

"You don't know where Nana lives,' Martha said.

"Well, they are calling my name so, I got to go," said Bethanne. They enjoyed the food and promising Nana to return very soon. Later she called Gabriel and Charles. They are excited and want to visit. She promised they would in person. Face time isn't enough.

Her parents and siblings visit. They reach the house about eleven o'clock. She is very happy to see her parents, especially her mother. She could imagine the amount of tears shed. Given another choice at sixteen she would shape her life differently. What a waste and unnecessary pain. This wisdom is not for her but for someone else and hopes she can pass it on. Her siblings are all grown up. They have done well academically. Johathan declares he is too handsome to settle down yet. He can't afford to deprive the world of his wonderful physique, showing off is rock solid abs. Yvonne finished her RN and is doing a bachelors in Pediatric care and Denise finished her teaching degree from Medgar Evers and specializing in early childhood education. She is engaged. Her fiancé is at

Colombia Seminary. She hugged and kissed her mother for so long. She felt like a kid again. She didn't think it was possible to miss the comfort of a mother so. She missed her dad too.

Dinner was a wonderful affair. Grandma is extra warm and pleasant and over- feeding everyone. There is merrymaking and music and competing conversations. She is happy and postpones telling her mother everything. She will do it on Saturday when they are alone. This is celebration time. Also, Charlotte comes, and she explains the situation and what she needs her to do. Charlotte graciously accepts though given the option to refuse. On Saturday she tells her mother every last detail; pregnancy, near abortion, Sisters of Mercy, the adoption of her baby girl and the theft of her son and finding him. She shows the pictures of the children and promised to take her to the park to see Gabriel play soccer. He's at the far side from them playing and she does not want to interrupt and leaves. Martha marvels at the illusion. The conversation with her mother seemed so real. She got cold feet. She is a big chicken. What kind of Christian is she?

Two months after her return home Det. Woods confirmed the request made from the lab might've been processed, but not in the case file. He will contact the crime lab because everything would've been preserved. Likewise, they will test her shirt again because, there was a drop of blood that doesn't belong to her or the Judge. There are many discrepancies with the case. So, Charlotte is made aware and fights to get the case reopened. It was a challenge but with Det. Woods revelation and a new ADA whose ear Charlotte has, decides to review the case/ record.

The evidence of DNA was done but never revealed because it exonerated her completely, beyond reasonable doubt. Because he was a prominent figure and there was political pressure to find the perp they rushed to judgement. There was the witness that told cops he saw someone running and the time Martha passed could not have stabbed the

Judge, He was not on the witness list. His statement was buried. There was no mention of the wound on her forearm- that it was defensive wound. Martha insists she wants DNA to be the tool to erase her conviction. The skin under Judge Frondes' nail matched the drop of blood on her shirt. She is cleared. She is free. No more PO, no more parole visits. She wonders at evil men so hungry for power and position sacrifices anyone for their grand ambition. The Mayor and Governor need the murder solved and prosecuted. Find a lamb; thus, she was sacrificed.

Epilogue

Things move so fast that Martha is impressed by Charlotte's tenacity. When the judge reviewed the case, he was angry. The ADA apologized to the court and Martha; they cannot give her back the ten years she spent in jail. Martha hugs Charlotte tightly and thanks her. 'This one is on me cuz,' Charlotte whispers. Martha walks out, goes home and soaks in the tub. She thanks God for seeing her through- smoothing the path for her exoneration.

She makes the six o'clock news on all networks as Charlotte and Hethe ADA held a joint press conference explaining that evidence was overlooked and that DNA definitely proves she did not kill Judge Earle Bradford Frontes. He also offered a public apology from his office, even if it cannot compensate her for ten years in jail. WASP office was buzzing and Gabriel and Charles chanted Auntie Marty free and danced. Their parents could not contain them. They got Auntie Marty back. Sasha and Keisha shook their heads at the teenage ingrates. Always Auntie Marty!

As a picture of Martha flashed on the screen young Sarai stared. The lady is striking but did they say cleared of murder. The lady looks familiar. She has a resemblance to someone she knows but who? Gabrie/ Peter is going into his bedroom stops. He sees Martha's picture. That is the lady from the park. He is sure of it. She's pretty too. That day in the park the fellows wanted to know who she was and if related. He felt a connection with her. She looked at him as if memorizing his face. And later that night her face floats in his vision. He went to sleep with her in his mind; such a beautiful lady. And in his dreams, she was watching him play in the park. Catch me mom…

About the Author

Claudette H. McLennon is a migrant from Jamaica who settled in New York for many years. She is an avid reader of romance novels, mysteries, and spy thrillers. She has an intimate and long-standing love affair with books. She loves the Bible stories as well as the Hardy Boys stories told her by her siblings. This sparked a love for writing stories. Hence, this story is the lively imagination of a teenager translated and brought to life forty years later.

This love of writing also led to publishing Ode to Lillet Rose, a book of poetry, and her first novel Sins of the Parents (due 2022). Currently retired, she is committed to writing more novels/ poetry. When not working as part-time Mary Kay consultant, she enjoys listening to music, doing crossword puzzles, doodling, arts and crafts, and light cooking.